THE O
OF THE ROD

THE ORDER OF THE ROD

A classic of Victorian erotica

MARGARET ANSON

SENATE

The Order of the Rod

Previously published in 1969 by Canova Press Ltd, London

This paperback edition published in 1997 by Senate,
an imprint of Random House UK Ltd, Random House,
20 Vauxhall Bridge Road, London SW1V 2SA.

Copyright © Canova Press Ltd / Luxor Press Ltd 1969

ISBN 1 85958 502 7

Printed and bound in Great Britain by
Cox & Wyman, Reading, Berkshire

CONTENTS

LETTER I
The Chateau de Floris   15

LETTER II
The Initiatory Ceremony   29

LETTER III
The Fair Flagellants   39

LETTER IV
Training a Page   49

LETTER V
A Remarkable Religieuse   71

LETTER VI
Preparing for a Sensation   89

LETTER VII
The Whipping of Cupid   105
A Conjugal Scene

LETTER VIII
The Woman in White   125
Mlle. Loupe
A Roland for an Oliver

LETTER IX
    Fanciful Flogging   143

LETTER X
    The Princess's Story   155

LETTER XI
    A Profitable Pupil   165

LETTER XII
    "Which ends this Strange Eventful
        History"   179

INTRODUCTION

The Victorians, for all their vaunted concern with propriety and a stifling sense of what was and was not acceptable, were nothing less than human in their concern with all aspects of sex and its expression. It is interesting to speculate that this entrenched concern was perhaps intensified by the very fact that all outward aspects of Victorian propriety were aimed to suppress and hide anything that smacked of the sexual. There is, after all, hardly a better way of rousing man's insatiable curiosity than to forbid him access to some area of life, some information or behaviour. And thus, beneath the stringently proper surface of Victorian society, there was created a veritable inferno of erotic practices and officially forbidden delights.

Above all, the Victorians were fascinated to the point of obsession by the subject of flagellation. In those sixty glorious years, the techniques of chastisement were elevated to an art, complete with its high priests and priestesses, its temples and a formidable literature. The motives behind this exaggerated concern are immediately obvious. In a society which suppressed, even to the point of refusing to acknowledge its existence, any form of sexual expression other than that intended for purposes of procreation, and which severely punished even the slightest infringement of this code, it is obvious that sublimated sexual instincts would manifest themselves wherever possible. Thus, in an age which prohibited the sight of a woman's ankle, albeit clothed in a stout stocking, but which permitted young men and women, boys and girls, to be chastised on their shamelessly bared buttocks, it is not surprising that the rod and sex became inextricably linked. Punishment, according to the devious social law-makers of the Victorian era, was essential to whip the filthy urges and lustful designs out of the young. Masturbation, that most harmless and natural practice, was universally condemned, and the poor adolescent offender was required to drop his trousers or to raise her skirts to receive just preventive punishment. Thus the buttocks became the symbol of sexuality. Always regarded as a private part of the body, their exposure at a time when everything else was hidden can have been little short of devastating to the beholder. But it was permitted, and thus the buttocks bared for punishment became an erotic object of unparalleled force, and the act of flagellation, always it must be remembered in the name of propriety, became a simulacrum of the sexual act.

Victorian erotica, of which there is a very great deal, is dominated by books extolling the virtues, techniques and practising of flagellation, and one of the most remarkable of these is here reprinted under the new title, *The Order of the Rod*. The book was originally published in 1868 as *The Merry Order of St. Bridget*, a title which has, perhaps sadly, lost much of its force and meaning in the latter half of the twentieth century. The contents, however, and its unusually fine presentation undoubtedly have not.

The man responsible for the publication was John Camden Hotten, an active, pioneering publisher and man of many interests who is probably best remembered as Swinburne's publisher. He issued Swinburne at a time when the poet was widely regarded as an obscene writer, and this act of literary courage has rightly assured him a place in history. He was, however, a very respected publisher who, apart from the more acceptable side of his activities, was also responsible for issuing a number of sexological books, as well as fine erotica such as the present novel. The bulk of the first edition was sold, at the time of Hotten's death, to J. W. Bouton of New York, a publisher who played a similar role to Hotten in the U.S.A. A French translation under the title *Une Société de Flagellantes,* with an introduction by Jean de Villiot, was issued in 1902 by the celebrated Parisian erotica publisher, Charles Carrington.

The author of the book is given as one Margaret Anson, but it has been responsibly attributed, by Henry Spencer Ashbee among others, to the author of another flagellation classic issued by Hotten, *A*

9

History of the Rod. This remarkable work is said to be written by the Reverend William M. Cooper, the commonest pseudonym of James Glass Bertram, a prolific writer of the period who produced, besides these indispensable treatises on flagellation, *The Harvest of the Sea* and *Out of Door Sports in Scotland*.

It has been claimed that Mr. Bertram was inspired to write the present work by an anonymous contemporary account of a female whipping club which met each Thursday evening in Jermyn street. This extremely amusing account certainly reflects the events of the novel itself.

These female foederates are chiefly matrons; who, grown weary of wedlock in its accustomed form, and possibly impatient of that cold neglect and indifference which, after a certain term, become attendant upon Hymen, determined to excite, by adventitious applications, those extasies which in the earlier period of marriage they had experienced. . . .

The respectable society, or club, of which we now treat, are never less than twelve in number. There are always six down, or stooping down, and six up. They cast lots for the choice of station, and after a lecture which is every evening read or spoken extempore, upon the effects of flagellation, as experienced from the earliest days to the present moment, in monasteries, nunneries, bagnios, and private houses, the six patients take their respective situations, and the six agents placing bare those parts which are not only less visible, but less susceptible of material injury, and also most exquisite in point of sensation, begin the courses of practice.

The chair-woman for the meeting accommodates each with a stout engine of duty, and being herself the *fugal-woman* in the evolutions, takes the right hand of line, and pursues the manual exercise in what manner, and with whatever variety she pleases : the rest of rank keeping a watchful eye upon her performance, and not daring, under a penalty of a double dose of the same nostrum, which is sometimes more than the offenders can endure, either at, or after the ceremony (sic).

Agreeably to the fancy of the chair-woman, sometimes the operation is begun a little above the garter, and ascending the pearly inverted cone, is carried by degrees to the dimpled promontories, which are vulgarly called buttocks; until the whole, as Shakespear says, from a milky white,

'Becomes one red ! !'

Sometimes the wanton, vagrant fibres are directed to the more *secret* sources of painful bliss ! sometimes the curious, curling tendrils bask in the Paphian *grove* ! and sometimes, as the passions of the fair directress rise, they penetrate even the sacred *cave of Cupid* !

There it is that the submissive patients generally, with one voice, cry out, 'It is too much !' and rising from their stations, express in the most feeling language, their several sensations.

The fair president now resigns her rod, and emblem and engine of her office, to whom she thinks the most adroit and capable, and together with the remaining five, take the several stations of their predecessors.

The course is recommenced with whatever additions and improvements the new performer pleases; sometimes the process is reversed, and beginning at the grove and cave already mentioned, with gentle applications proceeds to the swelling mountains, where the strokes growing more fierce and frequent, the second file of patients cry out in their turn for mercy!

The Order of the Rod is cast in a popular literary form of the time, *i.e.* a series of letters written by the pseudonymous Miss Margaret Anson to a female friend. This form is a happy choice, for the letter is an ideal vehicle for presenting tenuously connected incidents without arousing the reader's disbelief. Each letter can be of a suitable length, thus avoiding the danger of padding and, most important to successful erotica, it allows the author to get to the point with speed. Even more impressive, however, is the style of the book. Mr. Bertram is an extremely successful poseur. His letters not only have the chatty, relaxed flavour of an accomplished correspondent, but they truly seem to be from the pen of a woman. They are devoid of any vulgarities. The turn of phrase is generally happily feminine and Margaret Anson emerges from her letters as a very charming and complete character indeed.

These technical virtues, which are so often conspicuous by their absence in erotic books, have undoubtedly helped to make *The Order of the Rod* a classic not only of its subject, but also of its period. The author's knowledge of his subject cannot be disputed, but here again James Glass Bertram brings an unusual quality to erotica. Unlike most novels of its kind,

The Order of the Rod does not treat its subject ponderously. The essential, almost ritual, concern with the art of flogging is certainly there, but it is not presented with that peculiarly turgid earnestness which is lamentably so often a feature of such writing. There is a lightness, an almost merry tone about the elaborate ceremonies reported by Margaret Anson. This is a book in which the particular sexual delight of the characters has not ceased to be enjoyable. The author never loses sight of the fact that sex, even in this very specialised form, is a source of joy.

Nor is the book solely about flagellation. While never obscuring his central preoccupation, Mr. Bertram has added a wealth of detail about transvestism and female domination. As always, these aspects are treated with a lightness and charm which characterises the whole book. And, like so much erotica of the period, it is an excellently detailed record of the dress and customs of the period. Simply because it is a labour of enjoyment, a fantasy which is always credible without ever being mundane, *The Order of the Rod* fully deserves the high reputation it has enjoyed for so long, and will undoubtedly, in this new edition, repeat the success it has always received.

THE CHATEAU DE FLORIS

LAURA HOUSE, BAYSWATER,
April 10th 1868.

MY DEAR MARION,

I am sure you must have wondered what has become of me in all these years (three, isn't it?) since we met at Lord E's place. Perhaps you won't care to hear from me again, and will fancy I have forgotten our old friendship; indeed, my dear, it is not so, but I've been knocking about a bit, and seen the world. I've been in Paris two years in two different places, and learned as much in that time as many folk do in a lifetime. Cooped up as you are in a humdrum sort of place, with one old lady, you can have no idea of what goes on in livelier households. In my last place I was one of *six* lady's maids, all with nothing to do but to attend to some separate part of our lady's toilet. I entered her service from that of a grave austere woman with no ideas of colour beyond brown and grey, and a tremendous church-goer, so you may imagine what a change it was. I soon wearied of that place, you may be sure, and was glad when the Marquise St. Valéry took me into her service. The Marquis was immensely proud and very poor, but he bestowed his titles and position upon a banker's daughter, whose wealth was said to be fabulous. When she married and took her station among the *élite* of Parisian society, she made up her mind that she would be unapproachable in the matter of luxury. My dear, I can give you no idea of her magnificence or her extravagance. Her house, her carriages, her servants, and the splendour of her attire, were the themes of all Paris, and when she appeared in public she had quite a retinue of admirers and flatterers, while at home she seemed to hold a levée from morning till night. Her toilettes were the admiration of all the fashionable world, and her dressmaker had only to announce that she had anything in hand for the Marquise St. Valéry, to have her shop crowded from morning till night with ladies eager to get a sight of what the Queen of Fashion was going to appear in next. She was a large voluptuous-looking woman, with a splendid bust and arms, and almost anything looked well upon her, and for luxurious habits I never knew anyone who could approach her. I fancied I was pretty wide awake before I went there, but I learned things I never dreamed of in that establishment. If I had you with me for a day I could tell you such things! Perhaps I may put some of them into a letter yet. *Nothing* I could see done or hear of being done by fine ladies would astonish me now after what I have seen in that place as well as my present one. We were six of us lady's maids, and every one had her special duties: mine was her ladyship's head, and it was no sinecure, for her hair was her weakest point; it was neither of good quality nor luxuriant, and yet, when she was dressed, she appeared to have a magnificent head. This was my province, and she would change her style half-a-dozen times a day sometimes. You see it was no trouble to her, except to sit and have it put on; so she would wear Madonna bands in the morning, ringlets in the carriage, and a Pompadour coiffure for the evening. I had enough to do with it all. Another maid had the dresses, a third the underlinen, and a fourth took charge of her stockings and shoes. Then there was one over us all whose business it was to arrange the toilettes, and superintend the general effect, and woe to her if our lady was not pleased! With all her money, the Marquise had an exceedingly vulgar temper. The other maid had the charge of the bath and the linen belonging to it, and her post was not easy to fill. My lady was particular about her scents and powders, and was given to changing her mind at the last minute, and railing because water could not be drawn off, and fresh put in, in half-a-dozen seconds. Then she had pages I don't know how many; they seemed to be all over the place, dressed in all kinds of fantastic liveries: one to hand letters, another to fetch refreshments, another to be always in waiting, etc., etc.; indeed, there was no end to her vagaries, and for a long time

I wondered what she wanted with so many of them, and how she kept them in order. I soon found out. She practised whipping, as almost every fashionable lady does, and kept them in order with the rod. I dare say, shut up as you are, you have never seen anything of the practice since you and I were girls together at Mme. Duhauton's. Do you remember how we used to indulge in whipping on the sly, when Madame thought we were in bed? That was a very untutored way of proceeding. I have learned better since, and I can tell you that the passion for the rod is one which grows; I am as ardent a votary of whipping now as any of the ladies I have served, and I have had two mistresses who loved it dearly. Mme. St. Valéry kept her women and pages in order with the rod, and taught us to dread it, but she was not refined in her manner of using it; she would begin well enough, but it was sure to end in her getting in a passion. Many a time I have smarted well in her service, but if she hit hard she knew how to heal the smarts—a twenty-franc billet de banque is a good plaster for the weals of a lady's rod, and many and many a one I got from her. I might have made a heap of money if I had not been wasteful, for I've been with people who flung it about like dirt, and thought no more of five-pound notes than you and I would think of penny pieces. I was obliged to leave the Marquise at last—I could not stand her tantrums; the money was all very well, but there was no pleasing her, or the principal maid either, and as good luck would have it, my present lady wanted a maid, and was pleased with the style of the Marquise's hairdressing and so took me. I call her my lady still, though I have left her for a time, and come to live with her mother, a horrid old frump; the fact is, I am in a kind of disgrace. We had been paying a long visit at the Château de Floris near Tours, and there was nothing going on all day long but gaiety and fun, and the time passed quickly enough. My lady had to leave there; you'd see her name in the papers. She tells her friends she came home to recruit, but that's not it. My lord brought her off in a hurry, and sent me here—and what do you think for? For going in, with a lot more ladies, for a sort of club—great fun and *secret*—only ladies admitted— and how it got to my lord's ears was the funniest part of all. Anyhow, we had to come away, and he is furious. You will want to know what the club was about; well, it was made up of dressing, talking, and whipping. Yes, my dear, a regular whipping society, where the rod was used with all due forms and ceremonies, and ladies practised and submitted to punishment in every conceivable form. I thought of it all the other day when I came upon a pompous newspaper paragraph about the abolition of whipping in schools and homes, and the decline of the "barbarous" practice of the rod. Ah, my dear, newspaper folk don't know everything! I think you and I could tell them a little about it. But you wanted to know about the fashions; you've got them all in England,

19

my dear, only the English ladies are not so *finished* as
the French—they don't do things so completely.
When I was in Tours—and a funny old place it is—I
saw as much of the fashions as though I had been in
Paris. There was a large party staying there (at the
Château de Floris : it is a big old place, almost like a
town), and every day the ladies appeared in different
dresses in the salons, to say nothing of what they
wore in their own private rooms. I know my lady
spent a fortune while she was there; she would dress
in her own room, where no mortal eyes could see her
but mine, in lace and linen, embroidered silk shoes
and lace stockings, expensive enough to provide a
family with food and clothes for a year. The Count
de Floris spared no expense to please his visitors; and
the château, which was so secluded as to appear
miles from any town, was beautifully furnished and
decorated. The Count was a bachelor, and that perhaps accounted for some of the freaks of his lady
guests, who could not have ventured upon their
vagaries with a mistress at the head of affairs. The
drawing-rooms of the château were splendid; the new
blue was the prevailing colour of the draperies,
relieved with silver and satinwood for the framework
of the furniture. That the ladies' complexions might
not be tried, or the effect of their toilettes marred,
there were draperies of white lace very cleverly inter-
spersed, and the prevailing tint of the painted floors
and wallpaper was white also. The rooms were beautiful to look into of a night when the company were

all there in their evening toilettes. One which my lady wore at a ball excited great admiration, and envy too, for she had it sent down from Paris, made after a design she sketched for Elise herself. You know she is dark, and she chose amber for the colour of her robe; she wore the new pannier petticoat, which only wants a little more expansion to grow into the curious hoops of more than a hundred years ago, when ladies could have carried a box on each side of them; it is a very small affair at present, only meant to support the dress a little, but mark my words, my dear, it will *grow*—see if it does not. The bottom of it was frilled and edged with Cluny lace, and for bodice my lady wore one of the new slip bodies which form a chemisette and bodice in one. The upper part of it was covered with puffings of amber satin trimmed with lace, and sleeves of the same. My lady always wears *sleeves,* though it is by no means the prevailing mode here; she says that it is not modest to wear a string of jewels or a slight spray of artificial flowers for a shoulder strap, leaving the arm entirely bare; but it was not modesty, it was my lord! She appeared in a costume of that sort once, and he flew into a passion, and made her go and put on something more modest. My lady was very angry, for she is a fine made woman, and her bust and arms are worth looking at. But she pretends now to dislike the fashion. Her stockings were of silk, the new tint of pink—it is more like the faintest possible shade of mauve than anything else—with clocks up the sides,

and her slippers were of amber satin, with high gilt
heels. They were pointed at the toe in the Marie
Antoinette style, and had rosettes with ruby ornaments in the centre; the rosette was of the new blue,
edged with black lace and tipped with diamonds. My
lady has a lovely foot and ankle, and she knows it,
and is fond of having it admired; indeed, her legs and
feet have been painted, and modelled, and sung
about, by artists, and sculptors, and poets, and no
wonder. I've served a good many fine ladies and
beautiful women, but such a symmetrical calf and
ankle as hers I never saw. It was her feet that first
attracted the attention of a certain Royal Highness,
which caused so much scandal a year or two ago; my
lady is almost old enough to be his mother, but that
does not matter where beauty is concerned. She wore
an amber train, very long behind, with six puffings
round the bottom of the skirt; over that, a satin tunic
made in a very curious fashion. The front was square
and short, like an apron; the back was in three divi-
sions, a good way apart, with deep black lace
flounces between them, the bottom one going round
the front and along the edge of the apron. The
flounces were looped at the sides with large stars of
blue flowers mixed with diamonds and rubies, and
the head-dress corresponded. It was a curious
costume, but it suited my lady well. At the same ball,
a young lady appeared in a dress which had almost
no body : it was so bare that whenever she moved the
whole of her bosom could be seen, and was confined

on the shoulder by a wreath of snowdrops, cunningly fastened together. The whole of a most beautiful arm was thus exposed, an arm as faultless as my mistress's leg; it looked like veined marble, against a dress of rich pink silk : her arms were that young lady's special attraction, and she took care every one should know it. The turn of her neck was another lady's great point, and she was as careful to let no necklace or anything else come high enough on her throat to interfere with the exhibition of it; she wore a dress of rich blue, trimmed with white lace and pearls, and strings of pearls in her dark hair. The luxury and extravagance of the ladies would sound like a fairy tale if put in print, and I don't wonder at my Lord taking fright as he did, though my lady was not near so thoughtless as some of them. Our rooms were beautifully fitted up : the bedroom was hung with the new Paris pattern chintz—ugly enough I thought it, but it is all the rage; and my lord's dressing-room was *en suite*; my lady's was different, being all hung with amber and purple, amber predominating, and splendid white lace curtains. Her toilet table was beautiful to look at, for, in addition to her own service, which we carried with us, the Count had given orders that no expense should be spared to make her room as elegant as possible. Out of this apartment opened a bathroom, with fittings of white marble and grey draperies, relieved with blue and gold; it was warmed by a patent stove which also heated a small cupboard for warm towels if required. The windows were beautifully painted with arms of the de Floris, which device was also woven into all the napery used at the château. The linen was of the most exquisite description; the trimmed sheets and pillow-cases were of the finest texture—all woven expressly for the Count, with his cypher in the corners and a border of *fleur de lis*. Ah, the Count was a thorough gentleman, Marion: he gave me a present of a purse containing ten louis d'ors when I left, and—but that has nothing to do with it; ladies' maids have charms as well as their mistresses, and gentlemen have eyes. But I know you are dying to hear all about the club, and how it was set afoot. I can hardly tell you that, but it began with some nonsense in my lady's room. She had just come out of her bath one day, and was sitting in her chemise and a loose wrapper, for me to put her stockings on, when Lady C. knocked at the door. There were some queer tales going about respecting Lady C. and her maids; she was a passionate, proud woman, and had more than once got into scrapes for allowing her love for the rod to carry her to greater lengths in punishing them than they would quietly brook. Her present maid, Stephens by name, looked a regular tartar, and I don't think her ladyship ever tried it on with her. Lady C. started at seeing my lady half naked, and whispered something in her ear—

"Oh, nonsense!" my lady said.

"Why nonsense, my dear? It is universally practised"; and then she added something in too low a

24

tone for me to hear, and my lady laughed again.

"Send your maid away," says Lady C., "and we'll try."

"Go downstairs till I ring, Anson," my lady said.

"Not if I know it," I said to myself; and I did not go far, you may be sure. I guessed what they were going to be at, and I was not far wrong. I crept round to the door which communicated with my lord's room, and peeped through the keyhole. They had locked it, but the key was conveniently turned, and I could see all that transpired.

"Now for the formula," says Lady C.

"But where's the rod?" my lady asked.

"Oh! I'll soon make one, my dear."

With that she opened the window, and broke off some slender sprigs from a myrtle which grew outside, completely spoiling the bush by doing it. In a few moments she had them bare of leaves, and tied together with a blue embroidered garter, with silver fringe, which lay upon the floor.

"Too short to be of much use," she said; "but we'll try. Come, my lady, kiss the rod."

And my lady knelt and did it, laughing all the while; and then Lady C. pinned up her chemise all round, and gave her a good whipping across her knee. Not with the myrtle, though—it proved too brittle, and broke off in little twigs with every blow. Lady C. was at no loss: she didn't let go of my lady; but put up her great ugly foot, and whipped off her slipper. Such a slipper! it had done duty at more than one

ball, and was all frayed and soiled at the edges; she
was not like my lady, dainty about her feet in the
privacy of her own room, but went anyway, to
Stephens' great annoyance, who lost the reversion of
many things which should by rights have come to
her. I think I can see that old woman now, flourish-
ing that old pink shoe; and I could see by the
expression of my lady's face, that she did not relish
being touched with it. My lady had beautiful firm
flesh; her skin, though dark, was clear and smooth,
and every stroke of the pliable slipper raised a deep
red mark. I could see that they were afraid of making too much noise, and so the punishment was not
heavy, but my lady scuffled and screamed for all
that; and when I was called in, by which time you
may be sure I was a long way off, she was very
flushed and a little hysterical. I took no notice, and
she little thought I had seen all that went on; and
old Lady C. (the old gorgon) had her shoe on and
went away to her own rooms, looking as stiff and
stern as if she had never indulged in any pranks in
her life. I said to myself, "This won't be the last of
it," and I was right; for you know, my dear, how the
passion for the rod grows upon those who practise it.
It wasn't long before the same thing occurred again;
only, this time there were *three* ladies present, who
all took part in whipping and being whipped. My
lady had made a rod herself for the occasion, out of
some thin whalebone; and a stinging thing it must
have been, to judge from the fidgets which seemed to

26

afflict them all after the performance was over. And so it went on, till one morning I was made to dress her with more than usual care, and nearly all the married ladies in the château met in her rooms, and went in procession to the Count with a comical petition that the tabagie, which was a magnificently fitted smoking-room and in great request, might be given up to their use. Of course the gentlemen objected to give up their special den, where they could retire and enjoy themselves their own way, without fear of interruption; but the ladies had their own special reasons for wanting that particular room. I haven't, however, time to tell you what they wanted with it now; I hear wheels, and my lady will want me. I'll write again as soon as ever I have time, for what came of it was great fun. Meantime, believe me,

Your affectionate friend,
MARGARET ANSON.

P.S.—I shall write the next letters just as if I was still at the Château de Floris, and still engaged in the amusements of the day.

THE INITIATORY CEREMONY

My Dear Marion,

I haven't had a minute since I wrote last—my lady has been ill; neuralgia *she* calls it, I call it tantrums—but that's no matter. I have got a moment to myself again at last. Where did I leave off? Oh, I remember! about the ladies asking for the tabagie. They got it, and the gentlemen had to take another smoking-room. There was a great deal of joking and fun about it, and the Count offered any other room in the château; but they had their set minds on it, and they would have it. You see it was built out at the back, and had two anterooms: one the gentlemen used for their hats and sticks, and the other was fitted up as a lavatory. The tabagie opened on both of them, and was a fine room, all fitted up with deep crimson relieved with gold; the furniture was ebony, and the chairs and sofa backs were beautifully carved; there was a sort of dais at the end farthest from the door, covered with cushions, which was very useful to the ladies, for they made it a president's seat. It was some few days before they made all the necessary arrangements, and in the meantime the

29

Princess Z., a Russian Lady, and a great beauty,
went to Paris; she would not let anyone go for her,
though everyone (gentleman, at least) in the house
offered to go to the end of the world, if need be, to
serve her—and I don't wonder at it, for she was a
charming little creature, petite and winning. She was
a brunette, like my mistress, but not so dark, and her
silky brown hair fell over her shoulders in the love-
liest curls I ever saw; she would never dress it in any
of the new modes, for she was very proud of it, and
with good reason. She was said to have the smallest
foot in Europe, and, indeed, her slippers were more
like a child's shoes than anything else. There were
all sorts of stories about concerning her, and it was
pretty well known that she was too lovely for the
Empress's peace of mind, or the Emperor's either for
that matter; and that was why she was the Count de
Floris' guest instead of being at Court. She set off for
Paris in great style with her attendants; she did just
as she liked, and her travelling retinue was fit for a
queen. The ostensible reason for her going was to see
her lawyer; but that was not all, and the ladies
glanced at one another, and laughed, when she gave
it with all the gravity possible. They knew well
enough what she went for; and when they saw a long
box carried up to her dressing-room, they did not
launch out into any inconvenient curiosity, as some of
her intimate friends among the gentlemen did. The
day after her return, the ladies were to meet in the
tabagie for the first time; and the servants had a time

of it putting it in order. Everything belonging to the gentlemen had to be cleaned out, and the room scented and purified from every taint of tobacco. This wasn't an easy matter after years of smoking, but the Count gave strict orders: he said that whatever the ladies insisted on should be done; and between the gentlemen grumbling, and the ladies fidgeting, and the servants protesting, the nice old lady who was the housekeeper had a hard time of it. But it was done at last, and very thoroughly too, and placed at the ladies' disposal. A chair was set upon the dais, and others all round the room. A large ottoman, about the height of a chair, was wheeled in front of the president's seat; and two handsome branch candlesticks, which, by right, belonged to the hall, were placed on each side of it; and vases of cut flowers arranged on all the brackets which were fixed for the gentlemen's tobacco jars and cigar stands. The gentlemen laughed, and teased the ladies, and one or two went so far as to say to their wives that they *insisted* on knowing what it was all about; but they got nothing for their pains, save jest for jest, and repartee for questioning. At first it was only the married ladies who joined the assembly, but they were soon reinforced by the others, till at the time of my leaving the château all the guests, save a few of the oldest ladies, were mixed up in it. I knew what they were all about, for I "listened up," as someone says in a farce, and I knew that sooner or later they would want me, which they did on the very first

31

night. They all agreed to wear fancy dresses, and that, with some of them, meant just going as near naked as they could. One young married lady went as Una, without the lion of course, and really she went as near nature as she could: she had a thin tunic of some glittering stuff, and so few petticoats that I could see her beautiful limbs through it every time she moved—and she was a lovely figure. My lady went, that first evening, as la belle Sauvage, Mexican style: a skirt of feathers sewed on to flame-coloured silk, a flesh-coloured bodice, no sleeves, and a real tiger skin hanging from her shoulders, bare feet in sandals of skin with the hair on. She looked very lovely when her black hair hung loose over her neck and bosom, sparkling with drops to imitate dew; and it seemed a pity that only ladies were to look at her. When I had finished dressing her, and thrown a mantle round her, Lady C. came in hurriedly.

"We shall make a mess of it after all, without our maids," she said; "it will be fatiguing, and we shall require so many things."

"But it won't do to let them into the secret," my lady said; "I could trust Anson here, but I know you all can't say as much for your women."

"We *must* have someone," Lady C. said. "As President, I could not do without an attendant to—to—"

"Oh yes, I know, Anson will do," said my lady with a laugh; "she must be initiated, though."

They both laughed at this, and I felt rather

32

uncomfortable, for I had an inkling of what being initiated meant; but my curiosity overcame my distaste for the ceremony, and I curtseyed in silence. My lady bade me bring her several articles of lingerie from her drawers, and lay them out on the sofa beside her; also a handsome cashmere peignoir from the wardrobe.

"These will do," she said. "Dress yourself carefully, Anson, in case we want you downstairs; make your hair neat, and put on that little lace cap, and those things—*nothing more*."

I curtseyed again, and my lady went downstairs with her friend, leaving me to prepare for my coming installation as maid to these fair flagellants, for such I now knew they were. Their meetings had hitherto taken place in my mistress's room, where they had exercised the rod upon one another, but none of their maids was near, I took care of that, for I did not much like any of them. The French girls were not fond of me, because I was a foreigner; and the English ones were very jealous, because the gentlemen gave me more five-franc pieces and paid me more attention than any of them, to say nothing of the valets, anyone of whom I might have had if I had chosen. But that is not to the purpose. I took a bath, for I knew as well as my lady the best way to make myself attractive, and I knew, too, that not a lady in the château had a fairer or clearer skin than myself. I used freely the perfume and powder on the bathroom table, and did not neglect to scent the water as well.

I was determined, although my dress was to be so plain, that none of them should excel me in flesh-and-blood beauty at any rate. Then I brushed and scented my hair and coiled it up under the cap; I knew the ladies did not want a foil but a set-off to their beauty, so I did my best to make myself as neat and quiet-looking as possible. I put on the things laid out for me, and beautiful things they were too: a chemise of fine lawn, trimmed with Valenciennes lace and insertion; a soft white flannel petticoat worked round the bottom with silk; another of white cash-mere, very fine, with a flounce round the bottom edged with sky-blue velvet. For bodice I had one of my lady's embroidered ones, and over all the hand-some blue peignoir, with ruchings of white; no stays or drawers, and nothing on my feet except blue morning slippers, with tiny white rosettes. They were of watered silk, sandalled over my instep with blue satin ribbon; they were a pair of my lady's (our feet were exactly the same size, which was convenient for me). In this costume I waited the summons not with-out a good deal of curiosity and some dread. I knew thoroughly well what the sting of a rod was like, and it was not *that* I feared, but I knew how far the ladies could go in the matter of tormenting one another, and what might they not take it into their heads to do to me?

34

I had not long to wait, for presently Lady C.'s maid, Stephens, came in, and said snappishly,

"You're to come down."

Stephens was a cross-grained creature, whom we none of us liked : she was always interfering with our pleasures. She was in a cloak too, and I could see she was dressed something like myself, only not with such taste. Lady C. never could dress like *my* mistress. Stephens wasn't in the secret, and was inclined to be very cross.

"I wonder what all this tomfoolery is about," she said; "I wanted to have gone out this evening."

I knew, but I held my tongue. I hoped I should be taken into the room first, and then I should enjoy her surprise. We went downstairs to the tabagie, the door of which was closed, and one of the maids of the Princess Z. standing outside.

"How I should like to be you two," she said; "Madame says she can't trust *me*."

We were each put into a separate room—mine was the wash-room—and our eyes blindfolded with a handkerchief. It seemed to me a long time I waited, but I suppose it was only a few minutes, and then someone entered the room.

"Take off your cloak," a voice said that I knew for that of Mrs. D., an English lady, fat, fair, and forty, full of life and fun, who had been one of the movers of the scheme. "Now come with me."

The door of the tabagie was opened, and she led

me in; then it was shut and locked, and I heard the sound of suppressed laughter all around me.

Then a voice from the end of the room called: "Silence, if you please, ladies!" and three knocks sounded on a table, and the same voice asked: "Who comes there?"

Prompted by Mrs. D., I answered, "A candidate for a place in the Merry Order of St. Bridget."

"Are you prepared to serve the Merry Order to the best of your power, and to assist, as bidden by your mistress, in the ceremonies thereof?"

"I am."

"And do you bind yourself never to reveal aught that you see, hear or do in this room, on peril of losing your place without a character?"

"I do."

"Do you know the object of the Merry Order?"

"I do."

"Detail it."

Again prompted, I replied, "The wholesome and pleasant discipline of the rod, to be enforced by its members one upon another during their social meetings in this room."

"Have you ever been whipped?"

"I have."

"Do you promise to submit to such flagellation as the Merry Order shall ordain for you without rebellion or murmuring threat?"

"I do."

"Prepare her."

36

I heard more tittering when this order was given, and I could feel that Mrs. D. was shaking with suppressed laughter as she obeyed the command, and took off my peignoir. She pinned up the petticoats and chemise to my shoulders, and then, my dear, I knew what was coming. Then someone else took hold of one of my hands, and Mrs. D. the other, and waited the word of command.

"Advance."

They led me forward, and at the first step a stinging blow from a birch fell on my hips from one side, then from the other, till I had gone the length of the room. I screamed and struggled, but it was all in vain; my guides held me tight, and by the time they stopped I could only sob and writhe.

Then came another command, "Kneel down," and I knelt in front of the square ottoman; the ladies held my hands across it, and Lady C. came down from her dais, and whipped me till I hardly knew where I was. Then they made me stand up, and her ladyship said:

"Ladies of the Order of St. Bridget, do you receive Margaret Anson as a member and servitor sworn to do your bidding?"

"We do," said those who were not laughing.

"Let her see," was the next order, and at the word one lady let my clothes drop, and the other took the bandage from my eyes. I was so smarting from the whipping I had received that I could see nothing for a while, and Mrs. D. took me by the arm and led me

37

to the bottom of the room again. When I recovered myself enough to look about me, I saw a sight that the newspaper man, whose paragraph I mentioned in my last, never dreamed of, I am sure; but I must reserve it for my next, as my time and paper are both exhausted. Send me a line to say you have received this, and believe me,

Your sincere friend,
M. ANSON.

THE FAIR FLAGELLANTS

MY DEAR MARION,

I know you will be on thorns for the continuation of my story, to hear what it was I saw when my eyes were unbound after the unmerciful lashing I had received. As I told you, it was not very easy to see anything, for I could only twist and writhe about like an eel, and the ladies laughed most provokingly at the wry faces I made. At length I could look about me, and it was an odd scene I saw: all round the room the ladies stood, each one by her chair, with a rod in her hand. The costumes were all different and very fantastic, and most of their wearers looked more than usually handsome from being flushed with excitement. Lady C. stood on her dais as a priestess of Isis, with a wreath of bay leaves on her head, and her white cashmere robe looped up above one knee. She had sandals instead of shoes on her feet, and as she is ugly, old, and fat, you may imagine what she looked like in such a costume. Pretty little Princess Z. stood on her right hand as a medieval court page; her costume of ruby velvet and white satin showed off her beauty to perfection, and the silk tights displayed every muscle of her lovely legs. Mrs. D. had chosen a genuine old-fashioned dress of the commencement of the present century, in which she looked very funny, with the waist just under her arms, and the skirts so tight, that when she sat down she was a spectacle to be seen. But I can't stay to describe all the dresses; indeed, the ladies changed them so often that it would be impossible; and I don't wonder at the gentlemen crying out at the expense of their secret proceedings. Every lady held a rod in her hand, made of lithe and strong twigs, tied up with ribbons which corresponded with the colours of her dress. It was to procure these that the Princess went to Paris; to have sought them in the neighbourhood in such a quantity would have excited suspicion. On the ottoman over which I had knelt to receive my final castigation lay two more rods.

"Margaret Anson, approach," said Lady C. once more, and I went timidly forward, wondering whether any more whipping was in store for me.

"Kneel down."

I knelt, and she presented me with a rod, and informed me that I was now a servitor of the Merry Order of St. Bridget—allowed to join their ceremonies, and bound to do their bidding; and then I was made to go and stand at the bottom of the room ready to do to the next comer as the ladies had done to me. My dear, it nearly cured my smarts to think who the next comer was—that old cross-patch, Lady C.'s maid. There she was waiting in the dark all this time in a pretty humour; and I slyly felt the twigs of the rod I held to see that they were all separate and in order for a good stinging blow. Mine would be the first stroke, and I was resolved that it should pay a good many little debts I owed her. My lady was the messenger this time, and I knew she would do her best to frighten Stephens, for she did not like her. If the ladies had laughed when I was brought in they laughed twice as much at poor Stephens. She was a tall, gaunt woman, who never had been pretty, with a sour, haggard face, which looked positively hideous with her bandaged eyes. She was dressed in some of her lady's things, but they were far too short for her, and the washed-out green peignoir only made her sallow complexion look muddier than ever. She was terribly bewildered, and when the order "Prepare her" came from her mistress, and she felt the ladies' hands about her dress, she gave a great jump and a scream, and struggled to get her hands free. It was no use; my lady made a sign to me to hold them tight, and I did it with a will, I can tell you. Poor Stephens! kicks and struggles were no use, her clothes were as securely pinned up as mine had been in spite of her piteous outcries.

"Oh, my lady!" she screamed. "Where's my lady? She never meant me to be used like this! Oh, dear ladies, let me go, and I'll do anything you like, and never tell—no, not to mortal soul—anything I've seen or heard here!"

But the ladies only laughed, and told her if she did

41

not be quiet she should have her mouth tied up as
well as her eyes, and then Mrs. D. and my lady took
her hands and set off with her along the room as I
had been led. I thought some of the ladies would
laugh themselves into fits at the funny sight she was
when stripped; she had taken a bath as I had done,
but hers was not the kind of skin on which water
makes any impression, so as to look healthy pink and
white after it: it was all one uniform yellow-like
parchment; and her legs, my dear, they were nothing
but skin and bone, with great ugly knee joints which
stuck out in the queerest manner. My arm was ready
for the blow when the signal was given for the start,
and I let the rod I held come down with right good
will on her withered-looking hips, and the lady opposite followed it up with another given quite as heartily. For a moment Stephens stood stock still in such
utter amazement as I never saw, and then, giving a
tremendous howl, she fell flat on the floor and rolled
over and over in her fright and pain. How we got her
up I hardly know, for we laughed so, but she was
raised on her feet somehow and dragged forward to
the ottoman. She did not get half the whipping I did,
for she struggled and kicked so, and besides the ladies
were fairly exhausted with laughing at her. *I* had to
hold her across the stool, and she got it then pretty
smartly. When it was over she slid down to the
ground, and lay there twisting and groaning. Lady
C. was very angry, and bade her sharply "get up and
don't make a fool of yourself," but I verily believe

Stephens thought she had got into an assembly of imps, or that the ladies were in league with the Prince of Darkness himself—anything more ludicrously rueful than her looks when they took the bandage from her eyes I never saw. The rod which was given to her seemed to relieve her a little, and I heard her whisper, as she took her place and drew it through her fingers, "Wait till *I* get a chance."

But neither she nor I ever got a chance again. Our business was to prepare the ladies, to lead them up the room, hold their hands, present the rods, serve refreshments; in fact, *serve* in any way that was required of us. There was a universal vote for refreshments after Stephens' admission, and I was ordered to the door to tell the Princess's maid to ring for them. *She* was all curiosity, for she could hear a little but see nothing, the doorway was too well shrouded. She was a lovely, pretty creature, but not to be trusted; she was too great a flirt among the gentlemen in the housekeeper's room. When the refreshments were brought, Stephens and I had to wait upon the ladies, who seemed to have gained an appetite for their wine and biscuits by their frolic, and a good many of them were pleased to compliment my lady and me upon the neatness of my costume, and the good humour I had displayed in the ordeal to which they had subjected me.

Then they began to settle the rules of their society: they would meet again in four days, and every lady must be prepared to relate her own experiences, either in the practice or endurance of flagellation. If she had none, she was to be initiated forthwith, by being then and there flogged; if any lady's maid or page had offended, the case was to be laid before the meeting, and time and place appointed for punishment, where two or three chosen could witness the ceremony unseen; and further, if any gentleman practised flogging in his own apartments, his wife was bound to tell it under oath of secrecy. We, the new servitors, were further sworn, under divers pains and penalties, not to give our fellow-servants in the château a hint in any way what punishment awaited their misdemeanours. It was further agreed that any lady might take the place of another to be flogged, if they could so agree amongst themselves. There was a good deal of discussion as to whether the single ladies should be admitted to the society, but it ended in an almost universal decision that they should, Lady C. declaring very spitefully, though with some truth, that the girls of the present day know everything, and they wouldn't be any way enlightened or abashed at any experiences they might meet with in the Order of St. Bridget. Most of the ladies seemed to think it would be a new sensation the whipping of fresh young girls, and so the arrangement was carried universally.

Strangely enough, the Princess Z. was the only lady who had no personal experiences to relate and who therefore had to be whipped at the next meeting. A Russian by birth, she had seen plenty of whipping, but her parents had been too indulgent to flog her, and she was far too good-natured, and too indulgent withal, to whip her servants. She knelt before the president's chair, and expressed herself ready to suffer whipping at the hands of her sisters of the Order, and kissing the rod, resumed her seat. You may imagine what a chattering there was amongst the ladies between that meeting and the next; and the wondering what the Princess would wear, and how she would stand the whipping. She was very reserved about it, only saying her dress should be becoming the occasion, and it was. On the evening of the ceremony, she did not sit down with the rest, and the ladies took their places as usual with their rods. Mrs. D. was again appointed to fetch the Princess, and when she came in, the Merry Order started, one and all, and gave a murmur of admiration, for there she was in the garb of a penitent. A white robe of the softest silk fell from her shoulders to her feet, only confined at the waist by a thick gold cord to imitate a rope; no sleeves, nothing on her feet, and her splendid hair tumbling to her waist in natural curls. She had not an ornament of any kind, not a ring even; and if she had looked beautiful in full dress, she was ten times more lovely now. She held a great wax candle in one hand and a rod in the other, and never moved a muscle of her pretty face amid all the laughter which came from every part of the room.

"Who comes there?" demanded Lady C.

"An humble suppliant for the discipline of the Merry Order of St. Bridget."

"What is her offence?"

"Ignorance."

"Of what?"

"Of the discipline of the rod."

"Let her be prepared to receive it now."

I was directed to prepare the Princess, and I did so, revealing the most beautiful legs and hips in the world when I turned up the dress, and the exquisitely fine chemise, which was the only garment she wore under it. Then Stephens and I took her hands, in obedience to orders, and led her through the two ranks of ladies, who each gave her a blow with their rods, and I noticed that the ugly ones made their strokes twice as hard as the pretty ones. It seemed to me as though they were settling an account with nature for their own ugliness, when they let their rods fall on that white skin, from which red weals sprang with every blow.

She bore it wonderfully, only a start now and then betraying what she felt, though her rosy lips showed the traces of her teeth in more than one place. If she had never *felt* the rod before, she knew how to bear it; and it seemed to me as though the ladies tried their best to make her cry out. When she had been whipped up to the dais, Lady C. motioned them to pause, and put her through a formula of questions.

"Now you have felt the rod, are you prepared to admit the pleasure of receiving as well as inflicting chastisement by it?"

"I am."

46

It was hard work for the little lady to speak, but she screwed her courage to the sticking place, and did it bravely.

"And you swear to endure whatever punishment the Merry Order may impose upon you in the future?"

"I do."

"Then kneel."

She knelt as we had done over the ottoman, and Lady C., descending, dealt her several smart blows with her birch and resumed her seat.

"Rise, Princess Mathilde Z.," she said laughing; "now and henceforth an initiated sister of the Merry Order of St. Bridget."

I never saw such power of endurance in one so fragile-looking; after a few minutes of silent writhing she was able to speak again, and, curtseying, beg permission to retire. She was led out and taken to her room by two of the ladies, her maid not being permitted to accompany her. She returned before the meeting was over, a little flushed but quite calm, in a loose dress and a soft shawl. I hope you won't tell anyone what I write to you about the ladies and their doings. In my next I will tell you about a page the Princess picked up: she wanted a new excitement, and truly that boy has been an excitement to all of us. But you shall hear all about him in my next.

Yours truly,

MARGARET ANSON.

TRAINING A PAGE

My Dear Marion,

I told you at the end of my last letter that the Princess Z. had taken it into her head to have a page—a real article, no mock institution made out of a lady dressed up—not even a well-trained young gentleman from Paris—but a specimen of the raw material picked up in a field. The whipping meetings languished a little after her own installation; expectation was on the *qui vive* all over the château regarding the arrival of a certain M. and Mme. Hauteville, who were expected, and of whom all sorts of reports were rife; and, consequently, things were a little flat. None of the unmarried ladies had come forward or sought admission to the tabagie as yet. The ladies were disposed to be cross and annoyed, and the Princess's fancy was a diversion for them. It was a queer fancy, and gave me no little trouble. She was out driving one day with my lady, and was in one of her wilful moods; my lady was out of temper, but that was because her toilet was not so successful as the Princess's. That was no wonder, for whatever that little lady put on you thought it was the most becoming thing you had ever seen her wear. That day she was in gold-coloured satin and black velvet—a gold-coloured petticoat, with vandykes of black round the bottom, the points upward; meeting these a peplum of black velvet depending from a bodice of the same, with ruches of yellow satin. Her hat was a black velvet toque, with a yellow feather, which went from the front to the back, and fell upon her shoulders behind. She had black satin Hessian boots with gold buttons and tassels, and yellow gloves with jet ornaments. You would think this a sort of fiendish costume; but, my dear, she looked lovely in it. My lady was in pink and white, and was ghastly by her side. I never felt so disgusted with my own handiwork as I did when I saw the Princess step out of her room looking as she did. But this has nothing to do with the page. We had been into Tours ransacking the shops for some trimmings the ladies wanted, and were returning, when suddenly the Princess called out:

"What a lovely boy!"

"Where?" said my lady.

"There," she replied, pointing to the hedge. "Make him come here, Antoine."

Antoine got down and spoke to the young savage, for he looked like nothing else, and brought him to the carriage door. He was a tall, well-grown boy, looking about fourteen, and was lazily eating a great lump of the horrid black bread they use here. He had on a ragged flannel shirt, and a pair of old trousers, and what had once been a blouse; but there wasn't much of it left. His shirt was open at the neck and showed his chest; and his bare arms stuck out of his ragged sleeves. I could not help noticing how shapely they were, and the pretty turn of his bare feet and ankles, for he had kicked off his sabots, which lay in the ditch beside him. But the most remarkable part of his appearance to me was the dirt: I never saw anyone so dirty in my life. I should think he had never been washed for years. But the ladies seemed to see through that, and they looked at him up and down as though he had been some new kind of dog they wanted to buy. They asked his parents' names, and where he lived, and drove straight to the filthy little hovel, which was more like a pigsty than anything.

"I must have him," the Princess said, as they went along; "he'll make a perfect beauty."

"He'll take a good deal of *making*," my lady said, laughing. "Who is to operate on him? You can't touch him yet awhile."

"That's a difficulty—ah, I have it! I'll turn him over to Anson there—she has a strong will."

"And a strong arm which is more to the purpose; but here we are—these are your *protégé's* papa and mamma, I suppose."

A pair of horrid old wretches they were, quite willing to let the boy go, and horridly greedy after the money given them for their consent. I verily believe they would have sold him for a slave for a tithe of it. The boy did not go back with us: the ladies arranged that I was to fetch him after dark.

They did not want any of the men-servants to see him; and the pleasant task of training him was delegated to me. I did not like the idea of it at first, though I got plenty of fun out of it afterwards.

"I give you three weeks, Anson," the Princess said; "and after that, every mistake he makes, you'll come in for a share of his punishment; so take care and turn me out a page I shan't be ashamed of when I go back to Paris."

I thought neither three months, nor three years, would make anything of such a cub; but I was mistaken, as you would say if you could see Master Gustave, as he is called, now—Jean was his name before. Well, when it was dark, I went to the cottage and brought away the boy, taking him straight up to my lady's dressing-room, where the Princess was waiting to see him. He had evidently never been in a decent house before, and his wide open eyes and mouth were a sight to see. When he got into the room, he gave a sort of unintelligible roar at the sight of the ladies, and would have run away if we had not caught him.

"An unsophisticated innocent," my lady said, with a half sneer. "What is the first thing to be done with him?"

"Wash him. Anson, you will take him to the lower bathroom, and clean him thoroughly; I can't touch him as he is. Fifine will help you."

Fifine shrugged her shoulders as though she did

not like it; but there was no disobeying her mistress, and we led the boy out of the room.

"Get Saunders to help you," my lady called after us; "he will be more than a match for you if he turns restive."

Which he did as soon as ever he saw the water; he seemed to have as much natural antipathy to it as a cat, and he roared and struggled so hard that the three of us had much ado to hold him. He declared that he was clean; that he would not take off his clothes; that he would go home; and clutched his miserable rags till they fairly came off piecemeal. That he was a fine shapely lad we could soon see for his clothes gave way at every tug, and he was soon half naked. I saw Saunders pass her hand over his smooth firm flesh, when his shoulders were thus exposed, as though she liked it. Suddenly she drew her hand away with a scream, and dropped the dirty rag she held on the floor.

"Ah, the little brute!" she said, "he's all alive! Look here, Anson."

And sure enough he was—there wasn't a bit of his clothes as big as the palm of my hand that wasn't covered with vermin. What were we to do? Clean him we must. Yet it went horribly against us to touch him; and besides he kicked and struggled so. At last we got him down on the floor; and Saunders held him while we tied his hands and feet. Then we cut his clothes off and burned every rag of them. I had to do it: the Princess's maid would only pick up the rags

with the tongs; and Saunders contented herself with
looking on when he was once overpowered. When I
had done with his clothes, I began upon his shaggy
hair, and the murder I must have committed would
have put an army to the blush. I noticed that the boy
evinced less and less dissatisfaction as we went on
with our work; and at length laughed as though our
hands about him at once tickled and pleased him. He
showed very little shame at thus being stripped by
three women; but obstinately refused to enter the
bath. Saunders slyly took a rod from the table, and
turning him over her knee, administered a succession
of sharp cuts to his naked back and thighs, in a
manner that made him roar for mercy, and promise
to do anything we wished. I think astonishment was
the uppermost feeling in his mind at the proceeding:
that sort of whipping he had evidently never been
accustomed to, though there were plenty of bruises on
his body to tell of hard blows with more unmanage-
able weapons than a lady's rod. He went quietly
enough into the bath after this, and seemed rather
to like the contact of the warm water. 'Twould
take too long in a letter to tell how we washed and
scrubbed, and how often we changed the water and
got fresh, before we got him clean; but we managed
it at last, and turned him out upon the carpet, fresh
and sweet. The Princess was right he was a perfect
young Adonis. I never saw such limbs, or such fresh
healthy flesh, on any child, though child he could
hardly be called, being, as well as we could guess,

54

about fourteen. We rubbed him dry with soft towels, and dusted him with perfumed powder, at which he seemed mightily amused; and then some wicked impulse moved Fifine to give him a kiss. She had better not have done it, for the young savage retorted by throwing his arms round her neck, and kissing her rosy little mouth till she was fairly out of breath. This led to a regular romp between them, and Saunders had to interfere with her rod, and switch our *protégé* back to something like order. When she had a little recovered herself, Fifine burst into a merry laugh, and pointed to the boy, who was rolling a sofa blanket round him.

"What are we to do with him?" she said; "we have burnt his clothes! Is he to go naked?"

Here was a dilemma: there was nothing we could put on our shivering Cupid without letting the men-servants into our secret, and that we were forbidden to do. He laughed and jeered at our discomfiture; and, growing bold, declared he should do very well as he was: if we liked to look at him, he dared say our ladies would too; and a good deal more to the same impertinent effect.

"I have it," said Fifine at last; "I'll dress him. There goes my lady's bell!"

She ran off, and in a very short time returned with some clothes over her arm.

"My lady is impatient," she said. "She wants to see him; and says we have been long enough to wash him three times over."

55

"She doesn't know everything," said Saunders, with a grunt; "nor what we have had to do to get him clean. Are these things for him to put on?"

"Yes, there's nothing else for it—we can't take him about the place naked."

How we laughed as we dressed him! A pair of wide short drawers belonging to the Princess daintily trimmed with lace and open-work insertion, were put on him first, and securely fastened round his waist. They only reached to his knees and left the whole lower part of his legs bare. We had no stockings for him, and his feet were thrust into a pair of slippers of my lady's—those of the Princess being far too small. For shirt he had a short cambric dressing-gown of Fifine's; and Saunders insisted on adding a spangled tunic skirt that had been part of some of the fancy costumes worn by the ladies on some of their meeting evenings. He was the most comical figure when thus covered—I can't say clothed—that anyone could imagine. The tunic left a long margin of the drawers visible, and his legs sticking out at the bottom had an extremely odd effect. His face, now that the hanging unkempt hair was cut away, was very handsome— rather dark in complexion, with wicked-looking black eyes, and regular features, with a saucy smile upon them, as if he perfectly understood the way we women admired him. We threw a cloak over him and took him along the passage to my lady's dressing-room. What a laugh they set up, when we entered with the queer figure amongst us. I thought the Princess would go into hysterics; and my lady and Lady C. were not much better.

"What have you huddled him up like that for?" the Princess said; "I want to look at him. Come here boy—don't be afraid!"

"I'm not afraid," he said stupidly, though not shyly glancing at her white hands as she busied herself about the neck of his dress.

And I don't think he was, though he seemed rather bewildered at the splendour of the room and the ladies' dresses. He stared at the Princess in open-mouthed astonishment as she undid fastening after fastening till the whole of his queerly-assorted dress fell off except the drawers, leaving the ladies at liberty to comment as they would upon his well-developed form. And they did comment without the least restraint, and I could see that the boy understood *some* of their remarks at least, for a bright blush rose to his face more than once, and a smile mantled on his rosy lips and flashed into his saucy eyes. The ladies began to teach him on the spot, all naked as he was, how to bow and how to use his arms, and I could see that the mischievous little Princess took a sly delight in passing her dainty hands down his shapely legs and putting his feet into position. While she was stooping to do this the boy more than once made a movement as though he would touch her white shoulders, but, I suppose, fear kept him quiet, for he withdrew his hand as quickly as he had raised it. When they had amused themselves with him till they were tired, I was bidden to take him away and see him bestowed for the night.

"Bring him to my dressing-room in the morning," the Princess said; "Fifine will tell you when I am ready."

"And don't teach him anything but his *duties*," snapped out Lady C. "He'll be a pretty apt scholar at any sort of mischief, or I'm very much mistaken."

I spent a good deal of the evening in trying to teach him how to salute the ladies, how to enter a room, how to present anything kneeling, etc., etc., and I am bound to say I found him a very apt pupil. He was naturally graceful, and as long as he did not open his mouth he did very well; when he did he spoiled the effect of everything with his dreadful Touraine patois. However, one cannot do everything at once, and it was something to have him clean and willing to learn. I made him let me trim his hair, and brush and part it, and really he had a lovely head when it was done. Fifine came to us after a while with a blue and silver suit, in a kind of Swiss style, which she said Her Highness said he was to wear; and just to see how he looked, we dressed him in it. My dear, he looked like an old picture, with the dainty lace ruffles falling over his hands and the silk stockings showing the form and muscle of his legs. It made us all hug him and kiss him, even bony old Saunders, to whom he gave such a bearish hug in return that he fairly frightened her; he was gentler to Fifine and me, but then we had not whipped him. I

58

wondered what he would think when he was introduced to the Princess at her toilet; she was like some
of the women I have often read about, who look
upon their men-servants as though they were dumb
animals, instead of human creatures gifted with eyes
and senses. She would have her pages in her dressing-
room, and make them wait upon her at all stages of
her toilet; I think she liked to see their eyes fixed
upon her shapely limbs and to know that even those
boys admired her. She had parted with one who had
been a great favourite for some time just before she
picked up this lad and I could see that she meant to
install him in the vacant position. I saw that he was
properly dressed in the morning, and gave him two
or three more lessons before Fifine came for him, so
that he really did not enter the presence of the Princess so very awkwardly as might have been expected.
He started a little at the sight at her, for she had only
just left her bath, and was lying back in a soft fau-
teuil, with nothing on but a delicately embroidered
chemise and a soft flannel peignoir, which was un-
fastened all down the front. Fifine was rubbing her
legs, and putting on the quilted satin slippers without
heels, which lay read for her pretty feet. They were
of rose colour to match the trimming of the peignoir,
and had diamonds in the rosettes.

"Stop," said Her Highness, as Fifine took up the
shoes, "let him try his hand."

He looked rather bewildered, but I whispered him
to kneel on one knee as I had taught him, and he did

59

it much less clumsily than might have been expected. He took the dainty slipper, looking admiringly at the brilliant which flashed and sparkled in the firelight, and slipped it on to the white foot which Her Highness rested on his knee for the purpose.

"Very well done!" she said, laughing. "We shall make him a model page after all. Why, the little wretch!"

The last exclamation was followed by a smart box on the ear, which sent her new attendant off his balance, and laid him sprawling on the soft hearth-rug. Not content with the contact of his finger tips with her soft skin, he had the audacity to bend his head over her foot and kiss it. I think she was more amused than angry, though she had him punished on the spot.

"You shall whip him, Anson," she said, "and I have a great mind to whip *you* for teaching him too fast,—you girls have been allowing him too much liberty, I can see."

I begged and protested, and she laughed and let me off, only saying that she foresaw trouble in store for me, if that was the way I was going to instruct my scholar. She made Fifine undress the boy and hold him across an ottoman, while I whipped him. He struggled and kicked at first, but not as he had done the evening before, and did not seem to care about having his trousers taken down at all. The Princess looked at him with eager eyes, as his fine shapely limbs were thus exposed, and seemed half inclined to take the rod herself, but she didn't, and I was glad of it, for I longed to whip the prettiest boy I had ever seen. The first stroke of the rod sent him rolling on the floor, and made him roar out for mercy; but Fifine managed to hold him so that I could get at him and a sound whipping he got, I can tell you. It was very funny to see him dance, and kick. When at length the Princess signed to me to leave off, he was all over the room by fits and starts, howling and gasping like a wild animal. It was a good while before we could get his clothes fastened on again, he writhed so under the smart, but he has got used to it now. Her Highness made him beg her pardon, which he did with a face so blubbered with crying that she could do nothing but laugh at him, and then bade me take him away. When we were out in the passage, I asked him how he liked that part of his duties, and the little wretch actually winked at me (he had got over his smarts by this time), and said,

"I don't mind it much, I shan't care at all next time."

"Oh yes, you will."

"No I shan't if *she* does it."

"Who's she? Fifine?"

"No—the lady."

"You audacious little scamp, do you think Her Highness would touch *you*?"

"I'm sure she will."

I can give you no idea of the manner in which

61

that imp of a boy spoke; truly there wasn't much I could teach him. I thought to myself, "you'll get plenty of whipping, my fine fellow," and he did. Many a flogging I gave him in the week that followed with Fifine's help, and the rascal always paid us with kisses. We got very fond of him, notwithstanding his impertinence, for he was quick-witted, and very teachable and affectionate, in spite of his vanity; and long before his new clothes came home he was as vain as a peacock. It was about a week before the clothes came that were ordered from Paris for him, and all that time he was going about in queer fancy costumes, fairly turning our heads by his beauty. I don't think any boy was ever made so much of in so short a time. The livery was deep blue velvet with frosted silver buttons, the finest of shirts and cravats, silk socks, and thin kid boots. (The Princess could not bear anything like creaking soles, and tolerated only the thinnest of soles about her rooms.) After a little while she made no account whatever of having him in her rooms: she would let him go about her bedroom and hand her coffee before she was out of bed, and she rarely made her morning toilet without him. The first time she whipped him herself was about a month after she had first taken a fancy to him; I had done it often in her presence, and she had once or twice taken the rod and given him a few cuts, but she had never regularly whipped him with all the ceremonies. He had been very saucy to Fifine and me for a whole day, and he finished up his impudence by giving my lady an impertinent answer when she spoke to him in the evening. The Princess was by, and she ordered him out of the room, saying quietly, "I shall whip you tomorrow, Gustave." She kept her word. The next morning Gustave and myself were summoned by Fifine to her mistress's dressing-room. "You're *both* going to get it!" said the girl, with fun in her eyes, "Gustave here for being rude, and you Anson, for letting him be so."

"Then you ought to get a double allowance," I said spitefully, for I was annoyed; "he gets all his monkey tricks and wicked ways from you."

"Not quite all—but I dare say I shall get my full share some time; anyhow, I'm only going to assist today. Come along, we're to be Roman ladies' maids this morning, but the room's warm, thank goodness."

How I hated that freak the ladies had taken into their heads of making us wait upon them, just with one single article on, ready for any chance cut they might take a fancy to give us. However, they paid us for their vagaries, and it didn't matter much. We were soon equipped in the dresses the Princess had chosen for us to wear, and they weren't much. Fifine and I had short tunics without sleeves, and sandals on our feet. The boy's costume was even more scanty, for he had nothing but a skirt which barely reached to his knees, and no body whatever. I dreaded the whipping, for I knew how the Princess could use the rod; but there was no appeal, for my lady had given me over to her entirely, in the matter of Gustave, to do as she liked with me. The room was deliciously warm when we entered, and the air was fragrant with fresh scent. Fifine left us, while she went to attend her mistress in her bath. The door of the room was half open, and we could hear the splashing of the water, and now and then see the petite figure of the Princess as she flung her round limbs about in the perfumed water. The boy watched with greedy eyes; he seemed to have forgotten all about the punishment that was coming, in gazing at a sight so new to him. Presently the lady came in, wrapped in a large soft sheet, and reclined upon a couch, while Fifine rubbed and powdered her, removing the cap which had protected her magnificent hair, and letting it fall all about her shoulders. Then she attired her lady in a chemise of the finest lawn, with trimmings of Valenciennes lace and rose-coloured satin ribbon, and drawers, with lace ruffles at the bottom. Her feet and legs were left bare, only a pair to blue satin slippers, without heels, being slipped upon her blue-veined feet. Over all she had a loose robe of pale blue flannel, trimmed with white lace and satin; it was left open in front, and fell away from her knees, leaving her legs exposed. When all this was done, our penance began. The Princess was in the mood for arranging fanciful toilettes that morning, and sundry pairs of stockings and parcels of boots lay ready to be inspected. A large case had arrived from Paris for her the day before, and she had not gone over its contents yet. Gustave was made to kneel down on the

64

ground in front of the sofa, and support a round mirror, before which the wilful little lady had elected to try on the silken hose and dainty boots. I had a double office—to see that the boy kept still, and to hand the things to Fifine, who put them on her mistress.

The boy knelt very patiently while the contents of the case were one by one examined. He was evidently dazzled by the splendour of the costly dresses that Fifine took out one by one and laid upon the couches and chairs. The Princess had declared she was getting "quite shabby," and had ordered quite a relay of toilettes, and stockings and boots to match. Some dozen pairs of the most exquisite silken hose, and as many different kinds of boots, had been sent, and every one of these did she make her maid put on, and then hang the corresponding dress to see if they properly matched. To my mind, the prettiest of the dresses was rather a singular one, and one which, at first sight, seemed unsuited to the Princess's style of beauty. It was short walking toilet, of green and mauve; the dress and jacket were of emerald green silk, very thick and soft, trimmed and piped with bright mauve satin; the petticoat was of mauve satin, with green trimming; and the hat was a combination of the two colours, with a white feather; stockings of green silk, with a narrow mauve stripe; and fine kid boots, half Hessians, with gold buttons and tassels, completed the costume. The lace of the sleeves and chemisette was the most costly guipure, of an antique pattern, which accorded well with the quaint style of the whole dress. When she had the stockings and boots on she was delighted with the effect.

"They are the prettiest of the whole!" she said in ecstasy. "Everyone said I should look hideous in green and mauve, and just see there!"

Fifine threw the dress across her knees, and set the coquettish little hat on the top of her dishevelled hair, that she might see the effect of the colours against her brunette complexion. Certainly the result was ravishing.

"Take them away," she said; "I'll wear that dress this very morning to the croquet party. I'll put it on as soon as ever I have whipped that boy. Put down that glass, sir, and take off my boots."

Not only her boots but the stockings did she make him take off, and he made no mistakes this time; it was wonderful how quickly he had adapted himself to his new position, and acquired the little arts and graces so necessary to the making of a lady's page. This done, she made him bring the rod and kiss it, delivering it to her upon his knees. To prepare him was the work of a minute: it was only to fasten up the skirt he wore round his neck, and there he was almost naked. Strangely enough, he made no protestations on entering, but a queer light came into his eyes as the lady's hand passed over his bare shoulder, with a gesture that was almost a caress. Fifine and I held him down over the ottoman, and Her Highness administered a sound flogging to him, measuring

66

every stroke with a precision that I knew from experience only made the smart the harder to bear. He
roared enough now, and writhed and twisted, till at
length, after some dozen blows, he fairly struggled
himself free of our hands, and slipped on to the floor.
Then he clasped the Princess's feet, twining his arms
round her bare ankles, and looking up into her face,
implored her pardon. She did not grant it till she had
given him a good many rapid stinging blows, and
then she allowed him to get up. In spite of his roar-
ing and crying, I could see that the boy liked the
discipline he had received at her hands, and I saw his
lips on her feet too while he lay there clasping her
ankles, but she took no notice of it. When she had
done with him she would not let him go; she seemed
to like to see him writhe and twist, and ordered him
to bring the rod once more. It was my turn now, and
I knew she was going to whip me before him, but it
was no good to say a word. She rested a little, for she
was out of breath, and then she ordered me to kneel
and kiss the rod. I could have strangled the little
monster of a page, for the sight of me being prepared
for whipping seemed to do his smarts a mighty deal
of good, and he ceased squealing and rubbing himself
when he saw what was going on. The Princess made
him stand behind the sofa, with a rod in his hand,
while she whipped me, and told him if he stirred she
would turn him over to Saunders for another dose.
He had a horror of Saunders, but if she had proposed
to whip him again, or delegated the task to Fifine or

me, I verily believe he would have disobeyed her on purpose. I'm sure I heard him snigger when I knelt down, but when Her Highness turned sharp round, there he was looking so preternaturally solemn that she laughed herself, and there he stood as if he was carved out of a block of wood while she whipped me. I need not write of how she did it: she *can* whip; and it was all I could do not to slip down on the floor and roll and scream as the boy had done. I managed not to, however, and contrived to take the rod and leave the room without crying out, but my face was all working; I felt it and when we got into the passage that wretch of a boy pointed at me and burst out laughing. I couldn't stand that, my dear, and I flew at him and shook him, and boxed his ears till he roared more than he had done at the Princess's whipping. He has been respectfully afraid of me ever since; and though, since he has been downstairs amongst the men, he has learned a great deal of impudence, he seldom favours me with any of it. They can't teach him much he doesn't know already, for a more precocious boy I never saw; and yet no one can help liking him that comes near him.

I dare say you think, from the tone of my letter, that I have altered my notions about whipping; and so I have. While it was all punishment for me, to please the whims of the ladies, I could not see the enjoyment of it, or feel it rather, but now I can. Nor does the Princess feel half the pleasure in whipping me or Fifine, or even any of the sisterhood, which she

has when she gets Gustave across her knee to birch
him. I've seen her pause in her whipping, and pass
her hand over his firm flesh, lecturing him the while,
as if she would prolong his punishment for her own
gratification, and the little wretch keeps quite quiet,
and likes it all the while. As for me—well, there, I
suppose I may confess it to you, but I'm fallen in
love with the boy, or something very like it. I like
to have him near me—to be able to touch him when
I choose—to caress him when I please—and, above
all, to whip him when I can find occasion : that's by
no means seldom, for he is always in mischief. I sometimes think the little wretch does all sorts of wicked
things for the sake of getting a whipping from me—
for there's no mincing the matter, my dear, he is as
fond of me as I am of him. He knows a handsome
woman when he sees her as well as anyone, and I
don't think I'm so very bad looking. My feet are as
well shaped as any lady's among them; and the
Princess wouldn't feel flattered if she saw how her
page kisses them sometimes, when I have been
punishing him for some of his vagaries. Ah, my
dear, our whipping escapades among ourselves, as
girls, were all very well, but there's something like
enjoyment in having a fine strapping boy always at
your beck and call, on whom you can practise when
you like. There's real pleasure in getting hold of a
plump, firm boy like that, with a skin as soft as satin,
and laying him across your knee, especially when you
know that he likes it and you. Gustave's flesh is as

firm and rosy as a baby's, and every touch of the rod raises it up in red weals, like you see on a finely kept horse when it is lashed. He takes more delight in my whipping him now than in his mistress's, and likes me better than either her or Fifine, though the latter took his fancy at first. *Now* he says she's too *thin*—the audacious young scamp—and that he doesn't like *scraggy* women! Pretty well that for fourteen isn't it? But I must close this now. I'm going out with my lady. I'll write you again soon. Meantime, believe me,

Yours truly,

M. ANSON.

A REMARKABLE RELIGIEUSE

My Dear Marion,

I've been so busy, what with all sorts of whims my lady has taken into her head about her toilet, and that tiresome page of the Princess's, that I don't seem to have had a moment to call my own. I can't sit down for a minute in peace, but that provoking boy is sure to burst in, either with some message from my lady or his, or some nonsense of his own. He is as full of tricks as a monkey, and yet we are very fond of him. But I told you all about his beauty before, so I won't dilate on that now; thank goodness, I don't have quite so much trouble with him as I had: he minds me when he won't anyone else. I've not seen quite so much of him this last week or two, for another lady, staying in the house, has taken a great fancy to him, and keeps him with her continually. If the Princess tires of him, as I dare say she will sometime, he won't have much trouble in finding a new mistress in Mme. Hauteville. M. and Madame Hauteville are quite a recent addition to our party; and such a fuss was made about their coming! They are newly married, scarcely out of their honeymoon,

71

and are very rich; the best apartments in the château were given up to them, and redecorated for their use. I was quite surprised one day to find workmen busy in the handsome suite of rooms that overlook the private garden, pulling down hangings, etc., and the Count superintending with as much interest as though it were his own bride he was going to install there. He was always chatty and affable to me, quite the gentleman; and when he saw me peep in, he called me.

"Oh, come in, Mademoiselle," he said. "We are busy here; Mme. Hauteville is blonde, and those yellow hangings won't do at all. What do you think of that?"

He pointed to a great roll of purple satin damask that lay on the ground ready for putting up. It was lovely, fit for a queen's boudoir, and I said so, and went away, wondering who the lady could be for whom such preparations were made. I heard downstairs that same evening all about her. She was very young, not more than eighteen, and had come straight from a convent, where she had been ever since she was a child. She had a large fortune and a magnificent trousseau, and knew nothing of the world. This was what the servants said, and I heard the same from the ladies, who did not seem to care much for the addition to their ranks. I soon found out the reason of that: Mme. Hauteville was said to be excessively religious.

"Spends whole hours shut up in her room at her

devotions," the Princess said to my lady over the dressing-room fire; "thinks all amusements sinful, and seldom speaks in society, I hear."

"She won't join *us*, then," Lady C. said; "and I don't think she'll suit here at all. The innocent and ingenuous style is out of fashion now. It is only baby-faced women that can play it well."

"And that's just what she is," the Princess said. "Baby-faced is just the word; at least, I judge so from the Count's description. She is petite, he says, with golden hair and brown eyes, and a china pink-and-white complexion."

"And her husband?" asked my lady; "what is he like?"

"Oh, I've seen *him*: tall, and dark, and rather grave-looking. He is *the* Hauteville that distinguished himself so at the battle of Solferino. He is a personal friend of the Emperor."

Of course everyone in the château was on the *qui vive* to see these new arrivals; and it was a great disappointment to us that it was dark when they arrived. All we could see was a little muffled-up figure lifted down out of the carriage by a tall man, who seemed to take the utmost care of her; there was a valet, and a tall, rather stern-looking lady's maid, and an immense quantity of luggage, though that was not all, for more came the next day. There was a little Maltese terrier like a ball of white floss silk, and a big hound that looked tremendously fierce, but turned out gentle enough when we came to know

him better. I hung about, when my lady had done
with me, in the hope of catching a glimpse of the
new visitor when she went downstairs, and, sure
enough, I met her leaning on the Count's arm, her
husband following. She was as lovely as they had
described her to be, and more; such an innocent,
unworldly little face, I never saw. She looked as if she
had never had a profane or mischievous idea in her
little head, from which her golden curls hung in a
manner perfectly bewitching. She evidently cared for
no fashion in head-dressing except what suited her
best, and let her lovely hair wave as it would. Certainly, no chignon or frisettes would have suited her
little head: they would only have disfigured it. She
was magnificently dressed in rich white satin and lace,
with pearls on her neck and arms, and she looked like
a little fairy as she tripped along over the crimson
floor covering. She was holding up her dress in front,
and displayed her dainty little feet in silver embroidered satin shoes with high heels. I thought of what
the ladies said about her being so devout, and,
indeed, her face looked like a saint's, so pure and
passionless; but just as she passed me, she looked up
in answer to something the Count said, and I saw
something besides sanctity in her eyes. What expres-
sive eyes they were, melting and fiery by turns! I did
not wonder at the intense admiration her husband
seemed to feel for her; he looked at her as though he
worshipped the very ground she trod upon. He was a
handsome, intellectual-looking man, many years older

than his wife, dressed in uniform, and looking every inch a soldier and a gentleman. I watched them down the grand staircase with no little curiosity, and as I passed their rooms to go back to my lady's, the door was open, and the stern-looking maid was busy arranging her mistress's dresses.

"Come in," she said, as I paused at the door. "You are the Princess's own woman, are you not?"

"No," I replied. "I am with Lady ——"

"Ah, it's all the same. Tell me a little about the people here: are they sociable or stiff? I mean the ladies and gentlemen; I am asking for my lady. I always get on well enough downstairs."

I told her all about the ladies: how they were lively and affable, full of fun, and never done with all sorts of schemes for amusement and exercise.

"I am afraid Madame will be out of place among them," the woman replied; "she is so quiet, so retiring—she loves to be alone in her chamber: she spends hours there."

"What at?" I asked.

"Her devotions," curtly replied Sophie, for that, I found, was her name. "See here."

She pulled aside a curtain, and showed me a little oratory newly fitted up. I thought of the look I had seen in those soft brown eyes, and somehow or other I doubted the devotional part of the story. I did not say anything, but I helped her to put away the dresses, and exquisite ones they were, too; and we chatted about the company and the servants' table

75

till we grew quite friendly. Lifting the last dress out of an imperial, I came upon a long flat case, out of which an end of ribbon protruded. I guessed at once what it was; had I not handled such a one often in the Princess's dressing-room? But Sophie made haste to put it out of sight, muttering something about "Monsieur's fishing rod."

"Not a bit of it," I said to myself; "Monsieur never carried a fishing-rod in a dainty case like that, or packed it amongst his wife's dresses. I'll watch."

I did, and pumped Sophie as well, but nothing came of it. She was very cheerful and pleasant in the housekeeper's room, full of praises of her master and mistress, but somehow nothing could be got out of her. "She had been chosen by Mme. Hauteville's guardians to be her confidential maid," she said, and had only gone into her service on her marriage.

The ladies did not get much more out of the little beauty herself : she was very demure and quiet, and talked but little. She sang very sweetly, and was willing to exhibit her accomplishments for their amusement; but I fancy they thought her insipid, and wearied of her quiet loveliness. With her husband they one and all fell in love : he was charming, they declared, too good for her, pretty as she was. The little beauty reigned supreme on the first evening of her visit, but as the time wore on they felt her presence irksome. She was so very *good* they could not launch out in conversation, while the gentlemen sat over their wine, when she was present as they used to do, and they were never sorry when she withdrew, as she regularly did, to her own apartments, and left them free to use their tongues as they listed. The worst of it was that when she left the drawing-room M. Hauteville invariably vanished too, though where *he* went to was a mystery. Madame always shut herself up in her own room, and Sophie would take her work and seat herself in a large bay-window in the corridor guarding the door like a female dragon. She had the same answer for everyone who asked for her mistress.

"At her devotions," she would say, gravely, and we were obliged to be content.

If she was asked for her master, her reply always was that she had nothing to do with M. Hauteville, and if we wanted to know anything about him we could ask Adolphe. Adolphe was the valet, and I don't think anyone would ever ask him a second question about his master. He was very proud and distant, excessively polite, and that was all; we might just as well have tried to pump a log of wood or a stone as to get anything out of him about his master's doings. Well, this went on for several days, Madame appearing every day in the most ravishing toilettes (even the Princess could not vie with her in the matter of dress), and every day disappearing to her devotions in the zealous fashion which puzzled everyone so much. The ladies grew very curious, and tried to bribe Sophie to tell what it was that made her mistress so devout. Had she some dreadful sin on her mind? or was she vowed to so many hours a day before the altar? Sophie was dumb, and the ladies declared themselves tired of inactivity: they wanted to resume their meetings in the tabagie, and Madame Hauteville should be asked to join them.

"And I believe she will," Mlle. St. Kitts declared; "there's mischief in her for all her prudish looks, and, besides, there's more goes on in that room of hers than prayers."

"How do you know?" demanded the ladies in a breath.

"Oh, I was passing today. Sophie was looking out at the window, and I heard a noise that was vastly familiar. I don't think M. Hauteville would have been far to seek just then. But that grim maid came back to her post just a minute too soon."

"We must find out—we will!" said Lady C. "We won't have any private practice here. Can't you sharpen your wits, Anson? You seem very intimate with that silent waiting-woman of Madame's."

I told the ladies that it was no use trying to get anything out of Sophie; but they bade me try, and made me promise, on pain of punishment, to bring them any information I could get regarding the newly-married pair. I promised; and, my dear, I had a story to tell before I expected. That very evening I was sitting in my room mending some lace of my lady's, when Fifine came in.

"Where's Gustave?" she asked.

"I don't know," I replied. "Who wants him?"

"I do: I want him to go down to the lodge for me with a note."

"I thought the Princess said he was not to be sent out after dark."

"Oh, she won't know. I wonder where he can be?"

"He's in mischief, wherever he is. I haven't seen him since the ladies left the dining-room."

Fifine went away grumbling, and had to go her errand herself. I sat on, wondering where Gustave could be, and what he was at, and in a few minutes the boy burst into the room. If I wondered before, I wondered ten times more when I saw him: his hands and face were all smeared with green dirt, and his clothes were torn in more than one place. Luckily he had not on the suit he wore when attending on his lady, but one I made him wear when he was not likely to be wanted. I started up, and seized him by the collar.

"You little wretch," I exclaimed, "what have you been doing?"

His only answer was to laugh till he rolled on the floor at my feet, and I thought he was going mad.

"Oh ho, ho!" he cried. "Let me alone, Mademoiselle; I'll tell you presently. Oh, it's worth the risk I've run!"

"What risk? What have you been doing? What will the Princess say when she sees you? A pretty figure you are if she should ring for you."

"Oh, she won't! and if she does, I'll be ready in a minute. I say, Anson, I've found it all out."

"All what?"

"The 'devotions'. Such fun! Oh, my lady's a pretty saint, and says new-fangled prayers! Ha, ha, ha!" and again he rolled on the floor in an ecstasy of fun.

"But · where have you been? What have you seen?" I asked, quite puzzled.

"I won't tell you where I've been; but I've seen the prayers, I tell you. Oh, wouldn't my lady and yours like to have seen them too! I know they don't believe in Madame's piety, neither did I, and now I *know*."

"You aggravating little brute, tell me all about it this minute, or I'll whip you well," I said, shaking him. "You'll catch it for the state you've come home in, wherever you have been. What is it that the ladies would like to know?"

"What I've seen tonight. I say, Anson!"

"Well?"

"Are you game to climb a tree?"

"Climb a tree!"

"Yes, that's just what I've done, and, perched comfortably out of sight among the branches, I watched Madame Hauteville at her devotions. She didn't think anyone but the birds would be there, and the blinds were not closed."

So this was where he had been—up in the large tree which grew close to that corner of the château, and from which a full view could be obtained of the Hautevilles' rooms.

"You might try it, Anson," he said; "I'll help you, and I'll never tell; old Sophie may keep the door as she pleases, the window will serve our turn."

"But tell me what you saw, first," I said; "I'm not going to risk my neck to be hoaxed by you, and I believe you are telling me a pack of lies after all."

"No, on my honour, I'm not! I've seen what the pious lady does in her own room. She does not trouble the Madonna much, I can tell you; it's the rod she pays her devotions to, and not the crucifix, and beautifully she handles it too. I was almost ready to jump through the window and beg for a taste of it from her hands myself, when I saw how graceful she looked."

"You audacious monkey! But who does she whip?"

"Who? Why, M. Hauteville, to be sure! the gentleman who always disappears so mysteriously, and stays away from the company so long. Oh, they are a devout pair, they are! You should see him kiss her hands, and arms, and her feet, and call her all sorts of endearing names, when she has whipped him well. Try the tree, Anson; no one goes into that garden after dark, and you'll never get such a chance again. It's not hard to climb, and I'll help you up."

The lad's enjoyment of the affair was intense, and I longed to discomfit Sophie by finding out her secret; and yet the idea of me, Margaret Anson, climbing up a tree, and perhaps getting an ugly fall: how my lady would laugh when I told her! It was a great temptation, and at last I consented to try the next evening; Gustave was full of fun at the prospect.

"I couldn't have asked Fifine," he said; "she would have tumbled and screamed, and it would have been all found out; you may fall, but you won't scream, I know that."

"I don't intend to do either."

"And, I say, Anson."

"Well?"

"If you see anything very terrible, you can shut your eyes. M. and Mme. Hautville fancy they are alone, you know."

I aimed a box at his ears, but he evaded me, and ran off, laughing, to change his clothes, and all the rest of the evening he was provokingly confidential, giving me sly pinches and furtive grins, till he nearly upset my gravity before the ladies. He was in my mistress's room when Mme. Hauteville came in, a little flushed, but very pretty, and said, "Yes," very demurely, when someone said her exercises had been longer than usual. I thought he would have betrayed himself then, but he managed to hide his laughter by a cough, for which the Princess smacked his face, and ordered him out of the room. Well, my dear, to make a long story short, I actually did climb that tree the very next night. It was a wild freak, but the temptation was too strong to be resisted, and Gustave made matters easy for me. I was pretty sure of a couple of hours after dinner, and I put on a pair of trousers, which he stole from one of the men's rooms, and my dress skirt over them. Presently he came in.

"Come along," he said, "the prayers have begun, and all's quiet."

Not a soul met us as we went out into the grounds and opened the gate of the private garden. The night was as dark as pitch, and a bright glimmer of light came from the first-floor windows. A short ladder stood under the tree.

"Up with you," the boy whispered, "and hold on; it's easy after."

I wasn't a bit afraid, and in a few minutes I was sitting on a branch, where I could see right into the handsome room, with Gustave behind me, and this is what we saw: Madame de Hauteville, in an elegant undress, seated on a couch, with her husband kneeling at her feet. If she had looked handsome in full dress, she was inexpressibly lovely now. Her feet and legs were bare, except for the soft slippers into which her toes were thrust; her beautifully trimmed chemise was very short, and was the only garment she had on, except a white peignoir ruffled with Valenciennes lace, and adorned with knots of white satin ribbon. It was tied round the waist with a sash, but was all open at the neck, leaving her beautiful white bosom bare. A tiny lace cap was on her head, and her hair hung in masses over her shoulders. In her hand she held a rod, and she was rating the kneeling figure at her feet, with a mischievous look in her brown eyes, which reminded me of the first time I had seen her, when I guessed there was something besides piety in her little head.

"Isn't she nice?" whispered the boy behind me, with an emphasis which made me long to box his ears, had I dared to stir. "Look at her hands and arms, and her neck, ah!"

"Hold your tongue," I whispered; "you can talk by and by," and he was quiet for a bit. Presently M. Hauteville appeared to supplicate, and kissed the hands and feet of the little tyrant on the couch to no purpose: he was made to prepare for punishment by turning up the embroidered dressing-gown he wore. He had no more clothes on than his wife; and Gustave gave me a vicious pinch as we watched him thus prepare for the punishment we had both of us felt so often.

"Wait till we get down," I said to him, "and I'll give you such a taste of the rod as you won't forget." And I did—but that's neither here nor there now.

When M. Hauteville had received his punishment, he took his pretty wife in his arms, and half smothered her with kisses, finally getting the rod from her, and threatening her with it as he would a child. Then ensued a singular scene. She got away from him, and he chased her round the room, she every now and then defying him in a pretty saucy fashion, perfectly bewitching to see. At last he caught her, and, laying her across his knee, he whipped her as she had done him, using the rod lightly enough, but still raising red marks on the firm white hips. What more we might have seen I don't know, for just as he threw down the rod, and folded her in his arms, crack went the branch on which we were sitting, and we narrowly escaped a terrible fall. It did not break, and we managed to get down on to the next limb of the tree safely; but the noise had been heard, and out went the lights in the room above. We hardly dared to breathe, for the window opened, and M. Hauteville put out his head.

"It is nothing," we heard him say; "there is no one in the garden."

You may be sure we lost no time in getting away, though I did not escape without a fall after all: I slipped off the ladder and fell among some shrubs, which scratched my face and hands terribly. I was in a horrid fright when I got to my own room, and not all the washing and bathing I could give them would clear the scratches away. My lady questioned me so closely when I went to undress her, that I was obliged to tell her, though, of course, I did not say a word about Gustave. I let her think that I had thought of the tree myself, and scrambled up without any help. How she did laugh, to be sure, and sent for the Princess to tell her. That lovely little lady declared she would see for herself; and the very next time that Madame Hauteville retired in the evening, she and Mlle. St. Kitts were missing too, and reappeared later, with very flushed faces, and a great inclination to laugh whenever they confronted the handsome soldier and his demure little wife. All sorts of guesses were hazarded as to where they were, but no one but my lady and me knew that they were up a tree in the private garden, watching the pranks of the bride and bridegroom. Poor M. Hauteville must have wondered what made all the ladies laugh when they met him: I think the Count guessed something very near the truth, for his eyes always twinkled when the lady's devotions were spoken of. The sisterhood did not leave her alone long. My lady soon managed to let her know that her passion for the rod was known, and though she was terribly puzzled to think how it could have leaked out, she acknowledged it, and was received with acclamations at the next meeting in the tabagie as a right worthy sister of the Order. She is first and foremost in their vagaries now, and has a capital head for inventing any new nonsense for them to practise. I sometimes think she suspects Gustave and me, but anyhow she is very fond of the lad, who, on his part, seems to admire her almost as much as his real mistress, the Princess. As for the Count, *he* suspects I know, for the other day he met me in the corridor and put two Napoleons in my hand.

"To buy plaster for your face," he said; "myrtle twigs scratch horribly"; and then he laughed, and went away.

Now, it was right into a clump of myrtles I fell, so

86

he *must* know; but how? Ah, well, he can hold his tongue, and so can I; and I shan't trouble myself about it. I'll tell you if ever he says any more to me. Meantime, believe me,

Yours sincere friend,
M. ANSON.

PREPARING FOR A SENSATION

MY DEAR MARION,

I told you Mme. Hauteville joined the St. Bridget Society after the ladies found out that she practised the rod, but I did not tell you that Mlle. St. Kitts, who went up the tree with the Princess to see what went on, had already been received as a member of the Order. The discussion was long among the ladies, as to whether young people should be admitted at all; but they wanted a fresh sensation, and they agreed to admit her. It was a secret from most of them, and caused a great sensation when the President rose up in her place and announced that another lady desired admission to their Order. She did it with all due ceremony. I guessed what was coming, though I could see many of the ladies did not. Several of them had grown-up daughters, and had entirely negatived the scheme of allowing the girls to join their meetings. The young ladies were very very curious, as you may imagine, and used to torment their mammas terribly to tell them what went on in the tabagie of an evening. Many a present I might have had, many a pretty dress and bit of jewellery, if

I would have revealed the secret of those meetings; but I kept my word, for the ladies made it worth my while. The night of the whipping of the Princess Z., after she returned to the room (which, as I said in my last, she did, though flushed and feverish), and the ladies had refreshed themselves with wine and cake, Lady C. rose up and said :

"Ladies,—Sisters of the Order of St. Bridget, I hold in my hand a requisition addressed to me, as President of this meeting, which I beg to lay before you; another lady, staying in this house, is desirous of joining our Order."

The ladies looked at one another, wondering who it could be; there were only one or two married ladies left out, besides the old maids and the girls.

"Can it be Miss Sowerby?" my lady whispered to the Princess, "or Mlle. Loupe? There's no one else."

"I wish it may be," she replied, with a laugh; "to see either of them whipped would be great fun."

The spectacle of either of the ladies mentioned under the rod would have been edifying indeed. They were both of the pure genus old maid, forty, but neither fat nor fair—scraggy and parchment-coloured both of them. But it was neither of these. "Silence, ladies, if you please!" the President said from her chair, unfolding a note and reading. "Mlle. Geraldine Hilda St. Kitts presents her compliments to the sisters of the Order of St. Bridget, and begs the honour of admittance to their society. Mlle. St. Kitts is ready to take the oath of the Order, and to submit to the usual initiation."

The ladies looked at one another in dismay. That Mlle. knew something was evident; but what and how? I remembered when I heard the note that she was almost the only one of the young ladies who had not plied me with questions about the doings of the evenings when we met in the tabagie; but wherever she got her information it was not from me, and I am sure Stephens stood in too much awe of what might befall her to speak, however much she would have enjoyed playing the tell-tale on the ladies who had castigated her so severely. We were closely questioned, and every lady had the oath of St. Bridget administered to her afresh, but no one had broken confidence, and they were all fairly puzzled. Then Lady C. put the question,

"How say you, ladies? Shall we admit Geraldine Hilda St. Kitts into our merry Order, or shall we not?"

One or two said "no," but the majority were in favour of the candidate being admitted, and it was settled that she should be introduced the next evening, when they were to meet if it was wet; if it was fine there was to be a picnic in the day, and they would come home too fatigued for their ceremonies.

"But if we admit *her*," Mrs. D. suggested, "the other young ladies will claim it as a right; and I must candidly confess I should not like my girl to be introduced."

91

"Nor I mine," said Lady C. "We must manage to frighten her into secrecy somehow."

"I have it," said the merry Princess Z. "Let us horse her like they do boys. A couple of footmen would be famous."

"Footmen, Madame!" said Lady C., majestically; "admit *men* here! Impossible, you forget what you are saying, I am sure."

"Oh dear no, I don't," the little beauty answered, gaily; "and if the ladies assembled will allow me to address them sitting (for potent reasons I don't feel very well able to stand up again just now), I will explain what I mean in a very few words."

Lady C. graciously assented, and the little lady laid before the meeting a plan from which she thought a great deal of fun might be extracted—viz. that for the future, ladies undergoing punishment should be horsed upon the back of another who, upon that occasion, should be dressed in livery. She further proposed that the livery should be the punishment for slight offences against the rules of the club, and that failing any offender in the requisite degree, it should be worn by Stephens or myself. "And if we don't frighten Mlle. St. Kitts, it is a pity," she concluded, amidst much laughter and applause.

The ladies thought her scheme a very good one; but there was a difficulty—the livery: they could not apply to the Count for it, nor could they very well have it made, for fear of exciting remark. Mrs. D.

rose and called the attention of the meeting to this fact.

The Princess declared that she had thought of that before making the proposal.

"In the luggage that came for me today," she said, "there should be new liveries for my two men. I will have the unpacking done by my maid, and if the clothes are there, I shall confiscate them for our use; if not, we shall have to fall back upon the Moyen Age stores in the old lumber-room upstairs, though the dresses won't be so good. The girl will see through the masquerade at once."

The ladies drew lots who were to enact the footmen on the ensuing night, and the lots fell to my lady and the Princess herself, who declared that she must be a page, for she would be lost in a man's suit. So the other footman was turned over to a German Countess, who was tall and bony, and the rest of the ladies declared for appearing in Watteau dresses, half as men, and half as women. There were a quantity of costume at their disposal, besides their own splendid wardrobes, and they knew they could make a fine display. I believe they all wished for a wet day, and wet, sure enough, it was—no chance of any outdoor amusement. I had the note of acquiescence for Mlle. St. Kitts entrusted to me to deliver, desiring her to be in her room at a certain hour, when she would be fetched. She laughed when she read it, and said, gaily, to me—"Is it very dreadful, Anson? Come, there's no harm in telling *now*, you know."

93

But I wouldn't. I did so want to enjoy her astonishment, and, as well as the ladies, I had a fancy for seeing her whipped. She was a round, petite creature, very dark, almost a mulatto (indeed, she was of West Indian descent), with a clear, healthy red in her brown cheeks, and sparkling black eyes. There was a good deal of the Negro about her hair, which was short and frizzy, but very piquant-looking for all that, and her skin was the softest and glossiest I ever saw in a brunette.

"What must I wear, Anson?" she asked me when she had read the letter.

"Well, Miss, the less the better when you first go down; you can put on what you like after you have been admitted. The ladies mostly wear fancy costumes."

"The less the better, eh?" she said, with a merry twinkle of her black eyes. "Well, Anson, I have been in countries where ladies consider a necklace and a nose-ring the extreme of full dress for the finest court ceremonial. Is that the style of costume you would recommend?"

"Well, not exactly, Miss," I replied, laughing. "But it is a style that has its recommendations, for all that."

"H'm! I think I understand," she said; "but I don't mean to adopt it on this occasion. I know more than you think for about St. Bridget and her votaries, and I'll wear a suitable costume, never fear."

"You don't know everything," I thought to myself,

as I left the room, laughing to think of the fright that awaited the young lady, if no hitch happened to mar the programme laid down for the evening. Mlle. St. Kitts was very rich, and thought nothing of expense and towards evening she sent for me again.

"Will you dress me, Anson," she asked, "when your lady has done with you? It won't take you long, and I don't choose my maid to know anything about it. I've found a dress, and if I don't astonish your ladies as much as they mean to astonish me, my name's not Hilda."

Of course my lady gave me leave, and about eight o'clock I went to her dressing-room. There, laid out on the couch, was an exquisite tunic of amber satin, spangled and embroidered with silver and blue, and a pair of sandals to match : a cupid's dress, in short, evidently made for a fancy ball.

"Will that do?" she asked. "Minus the stockings, of course : you see, I know all about it."

I helped to dress her in it, and the effect was very fine. She had bathed, and her maid had attired her in a short chemise, exquisitely fine, and trimmed with the finest lace, with a narrow blue satin ribbon running round the top, and rosettes here and there along the ruche. Her hair was arranged to produce the best effect her short curls would allow, and a ribbon of blue and silver was run through it very artistically : her maid had evidently good taste, and she looked very bright and beautiful. As she threw off her soft dressing-gown, and stood with her beautiful limbs

95

fully displayed, I could well understand the ladies wishing to handle their rods in her behalf. Her complexion was almost as dark as a bronze statue, but shapely as any Venus that ever was sculptured. Her exquisite little foot rose at the instep with the true Arab bend, leaving only the toe and heel to rest upon the ground, looking almost too small for her childish stature. Her ankle was as slim, and her calf as perfect in shape, as any leg that ever was modelled by artist or extolled by painter, and the texture of her glossy skin was the admiration of all who saw only as much, and that is not little nowadays, as ballroom costume shows. It was a real pleasure to dress such a dainty bit of Nature's handiwork (such a contrast as she was to *my* lady), needing neither powders nor creams to improve her complexion, not any tight shoes or high heels to improve her thoroughbred little foot. The soft flesh rose up plump and soft between the straps of the sandals, firm and smooth as her round cheeks, and the beautiful leg looked more beautiful than ever when the high straps, with their glittering pendants, were clasped round it. Real diamonds glittered in the true blue rosettes which adorned the front of the sandals, and in the blue trimming of the tunic, as well as being worn in a thin line round her neck. A prettier Cupid never was seen in fairy extravaganza than that girl, with her Negro blood, when she was dressed for her initiation into the ladies' secret club. The tunic reached just to the knee, and had a half body of the same colour, which contrasted well with

96

the bright satin; round her waist was a deep crimson scarf with gold embroidery, neither long nor wide, but sufficient to add another well contrasting colour to the whole. She surveyed herself with a good deal of satisfaction in the cheval glass when her dress was complete.

"It is a barbarous mixture of colouring," she said. "No civilized creature would venture upon it; but I'm only half civilized. I'm ready for them now, whenever they like to send."

The ladies were quite ready, and I was soon summoned to my place: my costume for that evening was in the Watteau style, only plainer than the ladies—chintz and delaine taking the place of their silks and satins. My lady, in her footman's costume of blue and gold, and her powdered wig, looked so like a man that I quite started when I entered the room, although I had helped her to put it on. Gustave assisted at my toilette; the Princess liked to have him at hers and she sometimes complained that he was awkward, so I took him to my room to practise. I taught him how to put everything on, to fasten hooks and buttons, to hold a hand-glass, to tie sandals, and everything I could think of. My lady told me to choose a pair of garters for this evening from a box which had come from Paris for her, as my Watteau skirt was short, and I made him try them all on for me. You have no idea what beautiful things some of them were: velvet and satin, with mottoes and flowers embroidered on them in gold and silver, and rosettes, with real gems in them, and long fringed ends hanging down a couple of inches or so. I chose a ruby and silver pair embroidered with fleur-de-lis, and he put them on for me, telling me he was sure none of the ladies could show a prettier leg than me, and, indeed, I think he is right. I always garter above the knee, and that is one secret of keeping the leg a good shape; your knee loses its roundness if the garter is below it. I think Gustave half guessed what was going on in the tabagie; and, indeed, the Princess once proposed that they should admit him, and make use of him, but the ladies were afraid that he would not hold his tongue. I think he *would* : he knew the worth of his place. His mistress dressed him magnificently : he had suits for every possible occasion—for walking, for riding, for waiting on his lady at her toilette, and for being in attendance in the evening. For her dressing-room he had a loose suit of white cashmere trimmed with crimson, and a crimson sash—a sort of Greek dress in which he looked lovely; and when the other ladies borrowed him, as they very often did, they liked to see him in it. It was soft and colourless and did not clash with their magnificent toilettes. As for the demure little Mme. Hauteville, she was continually having him in her room, and would have him help to dress her from the very beginning; he told me one day that he had seen her in her bath. She was a most luxurious little lady; her bath was lined with magnificently painted porcelain, and the room panelled with looking-glasses, and hung with dark blue silk, which contrasted finely with her fair complexion and golden hair. She was fond of seeing herself reflected endlessly in the mirrors, and would dally in the water like a mermaid, splashing the scented drops about like a pleased child. She was the veriest little hypocrite that ever breathed, with her piety and her prayers. But all this is not to the purpose : I was going to tell you about Mlle. St. Kitt's initiation; I shall have to hold it over till next time. Till then, believe me,

Your sincere friend,
M. ANSON.

P.S.—My lady is gone out with the Count and Mrs. D., so that I have a bit more time to myself. I've been looking over your letter, and I see I haven't answered your question about Lady C.'s queer maid, Stephens. Who was she? you ask; and did you ever know her? Well, I don't think you ever did, and 'tisn't much of a treat to know her now, for she's a cross-grained old thing, in a general way. We got at her story quite by accident; we were talking about whipping one night over the fire, and she said :

"I told my mistress I never had anything to do with the rod till I came to her, but that was a fib : I helped at a fine flogging once."

"Oh, tell us about it," Fifine said. "Who was flogged, and who did it?"

"It was our ballet master at the Theatre Royal, Z."

99

"The what?" said Fifine, opening her round eyes till they nearly cracked, and staring at Stephens as though she were a ghost.

"The theatre," she replied composedly. "I wasn't always old and ugly, Mademoiselle, and there was a time when I could dance with the best. I was in the ballet there."

Fifine's astonishment was ludicrous to behold, and Stephens went on—

"Would you like to know what I was like in those days? I can show you; I kept my portrait, not from any vanity, for it is not pleasant to look at the ghost of your youth, but for other reasons."

She went off to her room, and presently came back with a miniature, painted heaven knows how long ago, of a very passable-looking girl in ballet costume.

"That was me," she said, "though you mightn't think it; and it was while I was engaged at Z. that I first felt the whip. It was the custom in the German theatres then, and may be now for aught I can tell, for the ballet master to have the entire control of the ladies in his department, and pretty strict he had to be, I can tell you. The Grand Duke was very particular about the ballet, and would detect the slightest inaccuracy in the dancing, or the least speck upon our tights or skirts. No expense was spared upon our costume, and every night, when we were dressed, we were passed in review before the manager and the ballet master, to see that we were properly attired. The latter used to hold a private inspection of his own first, and this we especially hated, the English girls particularly, who were not used to that kind of surveillance. He carried a rod, a lithe thin thing that cut unmercifully, and if he saw the slightest spot or crimple, swish it would come across our legs or hips, making us jump and smart for long enough after. One evening he was peculiarly aggravating—hardly one of us escaped a cut; he had us up before his chair, one by one, and inspected our coiffure, our ornaments, our skirts, shoes, everything. Then would come the order, "Raise your skirts, Mademoiselle"; and up they had to go, till he could see every bit of our tights right up to our waists. There were no drawers and tacked petticoats as are worn in England; nothing but the bare silk, which was of the very best, and looked thoroughly glossy and good. He was out of temper that night, and no one got off scot free. One or two of us he slapped with his hand, and I was one of them. He declared that the seams of my tights were crooked, and gave me a sounding slap; the girls tittered, and I sprang back, hardly understanding a word of what he said to me, when he pulled me across his knee, just as if I had been a child, and beat me with his broad fat hand till I hardly knew what I was doing. It was lucky for me that I had time to recover myself a little, or I should have got a reprimand from the manager for being flurried. It was no use complaining; the ballet master was omnipotent in his department; but we resolved to have our revenge, and laid our plans accordingly.

The next day was an off day at the theatre, but we had to be there for some trifling practice, and we knew the place would be clear of all but ourselves. We behaved with the utmost discretion, and went through our work "like angels" he was pleased to say. After it was over he went into the green room, and stood there for a minute or two alone. Now was our opportunity, and we seized it: two of the biggest and bravest amongst us stole in behind him, and flung a thick cloak over his head and face. He was a little man, and we were more than a match for him when once his eyes were blinded. In a very little while we had him blindfolded and hand-fast on the floor, writhing and howling, as only Frenchmen can, for mercy. He knew perfectly well who we were, but, of course, could identify no one in particular, and he alternately implored and threatened in the most comical manner. First he would call us "his angels," and declare he would never touch one of us again as long as he lived, and then we were little devils, and oh, how he would be revenged! I don't think he really knew what we were going to do till he felt our hands unfastening his clothes, and then it was all we could do, between our own merriment and his struggles, to get him prepared for the punishment we intended for him. At last we managed it, and got him pulled across a chair, and held tight down ready for the rod. And didn't we whip him! We had a lissom whip just like his own, and it passed from hand to hand with a will. We laid it on his yellow skinny hips till we were as tired with laughing and whipping as he was with struggling and shrieking. We left him there writhing and smarting, to recover himself as he could, and went home. At night he had to call upon the manager, but sent an excuse saying he was ill, and the next day at rehearsal he was singularly stiff and awkward in his movements. "He had met with a slight accident," was the story he told, and though everyone in the theatre knew the real state of the case, they were obliged to listen gravely. It did him good, and he pocketed the affront, and we girls came off better for having had spirit enough to resent his ill-tempered chastisements. And that was where I first saw the rod used, girls; and it wasn't yesterday, I can tell you."

"I should think not," said Fifine, wickedly, when Stephens was gone. "It must have been a good many yesterdays ago : to think of that old crab ever having been anything so wicked as a ballet girl!"

I haven't time to tell you anything about Fifine this time; I'll do it in my next. She chatters away without any reserve about her experiences, and they have been funny ones. Goodbye for the present, and mind you write soon to your affectionate

M. ANSON.

THE WHIPPING OF CUPID

MY DEAR MARION,

I can guess how impatiently you have waited for the rest of my story about Mlle. St. Kitts, and how she fared with the Order of St. Bridget. The Watteau dresses were a great success, but they were obliged to abandon the idea of half the ladies dressing as gentlemen for want of sufficient costumes of the style required; but they made up for it by the variety of colours, and the piquancy of their costumes. Lady C. old and ugly as she was, really looked handsome as she took her seat. She wore a tuck-up skirt of rich green satin over a crimson brocade skirt, and her hair was dressed and powdered under a hat of white chip, trimmed with crimson roses and green ribbons. Mrs. D.'s costume was dark blue over a maize skirt, which suited the Saxon style of her features and the colour of her hair exactly. But the greatest success was the two footmen, who stood with the utmost gravity on each side of the dais. They were both tall women, so that they looked middle-sized men, and their costume was perfect—high-heeled buckled shoes, silk stockings, white knee-breeches and waistcoats, and blue coats, edged with gold cord, and immense gold shoulder knots and tags. They wore white wigs, and looked a very well-matched pair of aristocratic footmen. The taste of the Princess in her liveries was everywhere remarked: they were thoroughly distinguished-looking, without being in the least gaudy. As for the little lady herself, it was her freak to appear as a page, and, in a suit of claret-coloured velvet, with sugar-loaf silver buttons, she looked the very incarnation of mischievous impertinence. Her dark hair was parted on one side, and rolled up into boyish-looking curls, and her tiny feet were encased in patent leather bottines of exquisite fit and shape. Her entrance caused a burst of laughter and applause; indeed, some of the ladies started, half afraid there had been some mistake and that a boy had actually got into the room. When the laughter and applause were over, and the ladies had sufficiently admired each other's dresses, they settled down into their places, and Lady C. gave the command that Mlle. St. Kitts should be fetched. The Princess's maid, who always attended outside the door, was despatched to bring her down, and Mrs. D. went out into the anteroom to receive her.

"I hope she'll enjoy it," muttered Stephens to me, grimly, as we stood waiting our orders; "it will cure her of curiosity for some time, I fancy."

Stephens never could get over the whipping she had received, and the chance of touching anyone else with the whip was a real delight to her. The ceremonial of the young lady's introduction was to be a special one, and I noticed the ladies handled their rods, which had been all freshly tied and trimmed, very affectionately, while they waited for this new object for their use. When Mrs. D. led the young girl into the room blindfolded, after the question "Who comes there?" etc., a murmur of admiration greeted her appearance in her fantastic but becoming costume. There wasn't a bit of timidity about her: she thought she knew what she had to encounter, but it proved a mistake. She answered gaily enough to the questions put to her.

"Are you prepared to join heartily in the ceremonies of the Merry Order of St. Bridget, and to further, to the best of your power, the amusement and pleasure of the meetings of the sisters thereof?"

"I am."

"Are you willing to swear never to reveal aught that you see, hear, or do in this room, now and hereafter?"

"I am."

Then followed the same questions which were put to me, and then Lady C. said, "Swear her." I had not been sworn, but I knew the ladies had gone through some form of taking an oath. A rod was put into Mademoiselle's hand, and, repeating after Lady C., she said, "I, Geraldine Hilda St. Kitts, candidate for admission into the Merry Order of St. Bridget, hereby swear to hold myself bound by all its rules, and to submit to all penalties imposed upon me by it.

I solemnly bind myself to answer any questions put to me by the president of the society, and never to reveal anything which passes at its meetings. I swear this by all the hopes I have of a good marriage and a prosperous and happy future, and, in token of my sincerity, I am ready to submit to whatever ceremony of initiation the sisters may deem necessary."

"Good," said Lady C.: "prepare her."

It was very little trouble to do that—only to fasten up the short tunic to her shoulders, and her beautiful figure was fully revealed. I saw the ladies look at her rounded hips and finely shaped legs with longing eyes, and, indeed, there was a pleasure in having such a firm smooth skin to lay the rod upon. She never flinched or shuddered, only saying to Lady C.: "Madame, is it against the rules to let me *see*?"

"Quite," was the only reply, and then came the word "Advance."

That she was hardly prepared for the first blow I could see, though she did not scream, but bit her rosy lip hard to keep down any sound, and, as lash after lash fell with varied force upon her firm round hips, she writhed and twisted, but managed to suppress any cry. When we had reached the president's chair, instead of making her kneel over the ottoman, I was ordered to advance and unpin the tunic, letting it down for a little while, and, still blindfolded, she was ordered to kneel.

"Mlle. St. Kitts will now tell the sisters of the Order *how* she found out anything about them," the president said, and there was a general titter. Mademoiselle was silent.

"She has taken the oath, and she will keep it," Lady C. went on.

"I will," replied the girl, trying hard to keep her voice from quivering. "At the back of the president's chair, under the hangings, there is a large closet; I was in there the whole of the first meeting of the society."

The first meeting! the one at which I had been initiated, and poor Stephens whipped. She doubtless remembered the way in which she had struggled and kicked, for I heard her mutter, under her breath, "The little viper." That particular evening Mlle. St. Kitts had been reported ill with a bad headache: some of the ladies had marked her absence from the drawing-room, and enquired for her.

"I locked that closet myself in the afternoon," Lady C. said.

"I unlocked it afterwards, and got in."

"With what key?"

"The key of my dressing-room door—the lock is a common one."

Lady C. looked angry; the other ladies amused, and the president went on "You saw everything?"

"Everything! The admission of the two ladies' maids, and the taking of the oath I have just sworn myself."

"Geraldine Hilda St. Kitts, you have acted the

109

part of a traitor and a spy! Have you revealed to anyone what you saw on that night?"

"To no one."

"You are an orphan?"

"Yes."

"From whence?"

"From the Island of Cuba, in the West Indies, staying here, and travelling under the protection of my aunt, Mlle. Loupe."

"Have you ever, except on the night you speak of, witnessed the discipline of the rod being administered?"

"I have."

"Ever suffered it?"

"Yes."

"Where?"

"At my father's estate of St. Kitts, in Cuba, where I practised it, with his permission and my mother's, when a child."

"And you like it?"

"I do, and wish to see more of the practice under the auspices of the Merry Order of St. Bridget."

I was ordered to the dais, to see that there was no one in the closet she spoke of—a ceremony which was never afterwards omitted—and I found that anyone inside could see very well all that was passing in the room, and Mlle. St. Kitts must have had an edifying example of the way in which elderly ladies and virtuous matrons could amuse themselves when they fancied themselves unseen by younger eyes.

"Will Mademoiselle tell the sisters of the Order *why* she kept her secret? Young ladies are generally prompt to gossip."

The girl's answer came quick and decisive to this question:

"Because I wanted to join the Order, and I knew that once talked about it would be at an end. No young lady under the control of a mother would have kept the secret."

"Then you confess to a passion for the rod, Mademoiselle?"

"I do."

"And will submit to whatever punishment the sisters choose to inflict for the crime of secretly watching their proceedings?"

"I will."

"Unquestioning and unmurmuring?"

Mlle. St. Kitts bowed, and Lady C. beckoned me, and bade me prepare her once more for the rod.

"What, *more* whipping!" she muttered in a low tone: but she made no remonstrance nor attempt to resist.

"Jenkins, step forward," Lady C. said, in an authoritative tone, and my lady advanced to the front of the dais and bowed in such a footman-like manner that the rest of the ladies tittered till rebuked by the president.

"The business is serious, Mesdames," she said, "may I beg you will be silent."

Mlle. St. Kitts started at the call for "Jenkins"; it

was an unfamiliar name to her, and she was at a loss what to make of it. By this time I had again pinned up her dress, and, in obedience to an order from Lady C., I made her step up upon the stool, over which I had leaned to be whipped. "Jenkins" came and stood in front of her, and the pretty tawny arms were guided round the neck of the supposed footman, who held them tight. A dexterous movement of the other gentleman in plush gave Mademoiselle a hoist up, and in an instant her ankles were secured by a soft silk scarf, and there she was, powerless. For a moment or two she took it all in good part (she had been horsed before, she told my lady afterwards), but it was only for a moment. She felt the cloth and buttons, and her chin rested on the horse-hair wig, with its black bag; it was a man whose back she was hoisted on, and she gave a loud scream.

"A man!" she cried; "Let me go! It is shameful! I will complain to the Count, and let him know what goes on in his house. Let me go, I say!"

If the ladies had tittered before, they laughed out now and peal after peal rang through the room at Mademoiselle's unavailing struggles and impotent screams. It was as much as Stephens and myself could do to hold her in position, and it was some time before Lady C.'s voice could be heard through the tumult.

"Mlle. St. Kitts has promised to obey our Merry Order in *everything*. Ladies, to your places, if you please. Jenkins, are you ready?"

"I am," replied Jenkins, in a voice which contended with muffled laughter, and the footman horsing the young lady planted herself firmly in front of the dais, and every lady in turn went forward and administered a couple of strokes with her rod. They did this with great precision, so that the blows had the effect of freemason's claps, and if Mademoiselle had borne the preliminary castigation bravely, she did not bear this so well. Half hysterical from fright and indignation, she struggled and screamed till she was breathless, so that when she was released from the grasp of the footmen, she could only roll on the floor and gasp. After a moment or two the order came to unbind her eyes, and, to her horror, she found herself face to face with two footmen and a page. Overcome with shame, she covered her face with her hands, and the president made a sign for the two supposed men to retire; then, addressing Mlle. St. Kitts, she said—

"Now you know, Mademoiselle, the penalty that awaits any improper spying into the affairs of our Order, and what you will subject any young lady to in whom you may, by hints or otherwise, excite an undue curiosity respecting it."

She then declared Geraldine Hilda St. Kitts a member of the Merry Order of St. Bridget, and I was allowed to take the poor girl away. Nor was it till the next meeting that she was undeceived about the footmen. She kept the secret capitally; not one of the young ladies could get anything out of her; and as for the cupboard, Lady C. made it impossible for anyone to make a spying-place of that, by having the door taken away. Mademoiselle was not able to appear again that night: her punishment had been much more severe than that of the Princess, and she was glad to bathe and go to bed. I went down as quickly as I could, and found Fifine scuffling with someone in the dark anteroom.

"You shan't!" I heard her say. "You wicked, spying little wretch, come out!"

"What is it?" I asked her, going in, and blinking with the sudden cessation of the light.

"It is that horrid little Gustave. I turned my back for a moment, and there he was, trying the keyhole of the door; if any of the ladies were to come out, they would lay the blame on me."

The fact was, Gustave had found out that his mistress had donned a suit which had been ordered for him; and his curiosity being great to see what she did in it, he had crept downstairs, and finding Fifine absent from her post for a moment, had applied his eye to the keyhole of the tabagie door, to try and see what went on within. Being caught by the lively French girl, she had pulled his hair and slapped his face, which led to the scuffle I had interrupted. I only made matters worse, for, when I touched him, he howled, and was heard inside. Stephens was sent out, and reported what the disturbance was about: and an order came out to blindfold Master Gustave and tie his hands. It was easier said than done; it took the whole three of us to do it, and when it was done, he sat down on the floor like a lump of lead. Mrs. D. came out and ordered us to bring him in, and we had to carry him and drop him just inside the door. He could not get the bandage off his eyes nor untie his hands, but he made himself as heavy and awkward as he could, and it was as much as we could do even to turn him over. In vain Lady C. bade him stand up, he wouldn't stir; and at last we carried him to the ottoman and laid him across it. In a twinkling his clothes were down and his shirt pinned up, and a sound whipping administered to him, every lady taking part therein. How he did howl and struggle to be sure, and how the ladies laughed! None of them spoke, so that he did not know who his tormentors were, and all his struggles did not avail to free his hands and eyes. Lady C. made him tell how he found out his lady had put on his costume, and he gasped out that he had been behind the window curtain of her dressing-room, and saw her put it on. Luckily, Fifine was present, so she had not *talked* about St. Bridget, or revealed any of their secrets. When the ladies had whipped him to their hearts' content, we were ordered to take him away, which we did, depositing him on the floor in the wash-room, which was pitch dark, and locking him in. No one could hear him there, and when he was released an hour afterwards, the tabagie was empty; no trace of the ceremonies or the sisterhood was to be seen; and he could make nothing of his adventure. He tried with might and main to get something out of me (Fifine knew nothing, so she could not tell), but it was no use; for I wasn't going to break my word for his vagaries, and I held my tongue. He got nothing by his curiosity but a good whipping, and it did him good : he was as demure again for several days after, though he would make saucy speeches to me about what he guessed.

"I'll find out yet," he said to me one day; "see if I don't; I'll come down quietly, and strangle Fifine, and then I'll take her place and get in."

"Fifine never gets in," I retorted.

"Then I'll strangle you," he said; "it's all the same; I'm not going to be whipped like that without knowing something in exchange."

But, my dear, he never did find out. The Princess told him the next time he dared to come near the tabagie, she would turn him out into his rags and dirt again within an hour, and he knew her well enough to know she would keep her word. But I must leave off now. I'll tell you all about Mme. Hauteville's installation in my next.—Believe me,

Yours truly,
M. ANSON.

P.S.—Our ladies are all in solemn conclave this morning in Mrs. D.'s rooms, and we are at liberty till they ring for us. I don't think anything to do with the Order of St. Bridget is the subject of their discussion, but I shall be sure to hear about it, whatever it

is; my lady couldn't keep anything from me if she
tried ever so. However, it has given us an hour or so
to ourselves, and I can scribble a bit more to you. I
really am very happy here on the whole, and Fifine,
whom you were asking about, is a nice, cheerful little
thing. I am sorry she is not in the secret of the
tabagie meetings, for I am sure she guesses about it;
and, more than that, she has been used to whip and
be whipped before she was a lady's maid. With all
her frankness and bonhomie, she has been tolerably
reserved about herself; and it was only by accident,
the other day, that I discovered what her history had
been, for she has a story, and a grave one, butterfly
little creature as she seems. One day lately, I noticed
that she seemed very absent and distressed—
frightened, as it seemed to me; but she declared there
was nothing the matter with her. Our ladies were
going to a grand party in Tours that evening, and
Fifine seemed terribly anxious to get rid of Gustave
and myself as the evening wore on. I fancied, naturally enough, that she had some quiet flirtation on
hand, and, as I never like my own sport spoiled, I
went out, taking the boy with me. We returned somewhere about eleven o'clock, and went straight up to
our rooms. Outside the door we paused, for unmis-
takable sounds of sobbing, mingled with the familiar
swishing of the rod, were plainly to be heard. It was
Fifine's voice, and for a moment we imagined that
the Princess had come back, and was punishing her

maid for some real or fancied fault. I felt sure that could not be, however, and I tried the door; it was locked, and Fifine's voice exclaimed in terror, "There's someone at the door! Let me go!"

A harsh, dissonant voice (a man's) replied, with a vicious chuckle:

"Let you go, my angel? What, just as I have recovered my lost treasure! No! let them come in, and see how naughty children are punished when they rebel against lawful authority."

He laid a wicked stress upon the 'lawful'; and Stephens, who had come up, seeing us standing at the door, started back.

"I know that voice," she said. "Where did he come from?"

"Who is it?" I asked.

"One of the greatest scoundrels unhung, I think," she replied. "A fellow that got into good society in Paris through lies and effrontery; he got kicked out of the drawing-room, and then tried to ingratiate himself downstairs. His name is Barbel, and he once wanted to marry me."

"Oh my!" ejaculated Gustave, under his breath.

"Not for my good looks, you monkey, but for a bit of money I'd saved. Luckily, I found out in time that he had a wife somewhere, though he himself did not know where. Here, M. Barbel, open that door," she added, calling through the keyhole.

"Ah, that voice!" exclaimed the man within. "Certainly my charming Mademoiselle, whom I have the happiness to recognize. Come in, and assist at a conjugal tête-à-tête."

He came tripping across the room as he spoke, and flung the door open, admitting us to a somewhat odd scene. Fifine was tied across a heavy chair in the middle of the room, crying; as if her heart would break, her clothes turned up with the utmost precision, while the ugliest old man I ever saw was administering a whipping, which had already been severe, judging from the state of her hips and her tear-stained and swollen face.

"You nasty brute, let her go!" exclaimed Gustave, springing to her side, and beginning to unfasten the handkerchiefs with which she was secured, while Stephens poured out the full measure of her wrath upon his head, calling him all the names she could think of, and shaking her fist at him in scorn and anger.

"Pardon, ladies; softly, young sir!" he said with an odious leer. "Shall not a man do what he likes with his own? This lady is my runaway wife, my chattel, my goods; and who shall forbid my chastising her when I find her?"

Gustave and I were so petrified with astonishment that we could only stare at him, but Stephens came to the rescue with tact and skill.

"Of course you can have your wife," she said, "and whip her twenty times a-day if you like; but not in another lady's rooms. This apartment is Miss Anson's, and I see she does not much fancy your company in it. Will you favour me by coming to mine?"

He hesitated a moment, and looked at Fifine, who sat with her head buried in her hands.

"Oh, never mind your wife!" Stephens went on. "You've hindered her from running away for to-night at least; a glass of wine would be no bad thing after your exertions"; and so speaking, she actually walked him off, leaving us alone with Fifine, who seemed almost beside herself with fright.

We soothed and comforted her as well as we could, and when she was calm enough to speak, we asked her if it was true.

"Yes," she said, through her tears; "quite true, I am his wife, heaven help me! but I hoped I should never see him again," and then, bit by bit, her story came out. I fancy a good many French girls could tell the same if we only knew. Fifine was by no means a lowly-born girl; she came of a good family, though poor. Her parents died, leaving her a little money, and she was placed in a convent, from whence she was taken by her guardian, at the age of sixteen, to be given in marriage to the man whom Stephens had called Barbel. That he was old, ugly, and dissipated, mattered nothing; he was the man chosen for her, and, as these things are always arranged in France, she took him, doubtless hoping that she should shake down into her new life, as hundreds of women do, without feeling her position too acutely. She reckoned without her host, however :

she was tied to a man without sense of honour or decency; and after being outraged as only such brutes can outrage helpless women, she fled from him and threw herself upon the mercy of the Princess Z., whose husband had known her father. That lady listened to her pitiful story, and took means to ascertain its truth, and finally allowed the poor wife, under an assumed name, to become her attendant.

"And I should be so happy," she sobbed, when she had told us all, "but for him; this is the second time he has found me, and no one but the Prince has any influence over him to keep him away, and he is so far off."

We asked her how he got in, and she said she met him on the previous evening, when he had announced his intention of coming, and declared he would claim her publicly if she did not admit him.

"And oh!" she added, in a terrified voice, "I don't know how to tell you, but things are not safe where he is; he has been in prison once, and—"

She burst into such passionate tears that our hearts ached to see her.

"We'll get rid of him somehow," Gustave said, encouragingly. "Stephens won't let him go blabbing— she knows him, she said; he made love to her in Paris."

"Go and see what has become of him," I said; and Gustave went, and presently reappeared, saying, "It's all right; stop with Fifine—my assistance is wanted yonder."

He stayed away about an hour, and then they both came back. Stephens had actually taken him to her own room, and, with Gustave's help, made him drunk!

"It was the only thing," she said, grimly; "nobody would suspect *me* of an intrigue, and he must be got rid of. When the Princess comes home we will tell her." We did, and she entered fully into Fifine's tribulation.

"He must be turned out of course," she said—"the brute; and I think, *I* can make him hold his tongue; in the meantime I leave him to you."

We took the hint, and, after seeing Fifine and her mistress to bed, we three went into Stephens' room, and when M. Barbel woke up out of his drunken sleep, it was to feel the smartest cuts that our rods could give him. We had fastened him as he had fastened his poor little wife, and I'll answer for him it would be a long time before he'd forget what sort of a whipping two women could give him. When we had done, I gave him a message from the Princess to the effect that, if ever he molested Fifine again, while she was with her, instant arrest would be his portion. He understood, though we did not, and became abjectly humble, and declared his willingness to depart at once. We let him go, and he slunk off; but his adventures did not end here: one of the men recognized him, as he was going out of the house, as a fellow who had swindled him in Paris, and administered summary justice on the spot in the shape of a good kicking. Poor Fifine looks very pale and distraught, but she will soon recover her spirits, for he is safe for some time: the very day after he left Tours he was arrested for forgery and robbery, and lies awaiting his trial. It would be no loss to society if they sent him to the galleys for life—the monster! To think of little Fifine having such a story belonging to her! "Still waters run deep," the proverb says; but I should never have thought there was anything below the surface in her. There's my lady calling: now I shall hear what the discussion has been about. It is sure to be something to make more toilet work for us girls. Goodbye till I write again, which won't be long.

Ever your affectionate,

M. ANSON.

THE WOMAN IN WHITE

My Dear Marion,

I promised to tell you about the installation of Mme. Hauteville to a place in the Order of St. Bridget. It took place at the very next meeting after I had caught Gustave and he had been whipped. There was nothing new to be done—whipping is whipping, and nothing can make it different. But the ladies resolved to have something fresh about it, and agreed that, instead of all having the orthodox rods, they should have as many kinds of instruments of punishment as they could think of; thus, one lady should use a slipper; another a birch, tightly tied; another a loosely-fastened rod, and so on. Mrs. D. declared for nothing at all: she would use the palm of her hand only, she said, "and if I don't make as much impression as any of you," she added, wickedly, "why I have forgotten my practice, that's all."

Mme. Hauteville made a very pretty toilette for the occasion; she was all in white, not a penitent like the Princess had been for her admission, but in the costume of a novice when she takes the veil. The dress had been considerably modified as being too flowing for the occasion, but it was all white silk and lace, and a lovely little angel she looked when it was completed. From head to foot she had nothing on that was not pure white. White satin shoes, with diamonds sparkling on the rosettes; white silk stockings, gartered above her round knees with white velvet garters, with satin rosettes; white petticoats—one of the finest flannel, embroidered with lilies, and one of soft lawn, with lace flounce. Her robe was silk, the soft noiseless sort that does not rustle, richly trimmed with costly Mechlin lace, and over her head she had a square veil. She had Gustave to assist at her toilette, and allowed him to put on her exquisite stockings, and fasten her garters and shoes. I could see the delight the mischievous rogue felt in doing it; his face flushed, and his hands trembled so that he could hardly clasp the silver fastenings. But Madame never minded him a bit; she seemed rather to like feeling his hands about her, and very nice hands they had grown into by now, I can assure you. He looked wistfully after her as we escorted her downstairs, but he dared not follow this time. Madame submitted to be blind-folded with a very good grace, though she tried hard to get me to tell her what was going to be done; she had such pretty coaxing ways that it was hard to resist her; but I did, and she went in quite unprepared. We led her slowly up the room, and at the first stroke of the rod, nearest the door, she winced, but did not cry out; the next blow she received was a stinging one from a slipper my lady held in her hand (she knows how to strike with a shoe, I can tell you), and she gave a little scream and a jump. "Oh, what is it?" she said, between her teeth; but the next stroke, a fair open-handed slap from Mrs. D.'s fat hand, made her fairly shriek out, and twist herself out of our grasp on to the floor. It *was* a slap, and rang out even above the laughter of the ladies, leaving a broad red mark on the white, firm flesh of the little lady.

"Stop punishment!" said Lady C. from her dais; "the applicant will answer the questions of the Merry Order before she is further whipped."

We led her to the ottoman, and she knelt over it.

"Angeline Marie Hauteville," she went on, "you promise to obey the Merry Order of St. Bridget in all things pertaining to their rites?"

"I do."

"And to answer all questioning from their president?"

"I do."

"You are accustomed to the practice of the rod?"

"I am."

"And have a passion for it?"

Mme. Hauteville bowed, but made no answer.

"Your husband joins you in the practice?"

Another mute bow, and the fair face turned fiery red, no doubt at the thought of that same private practice, and how it must have been seen by someone.

"State to the Merry Order how you became

acquainted with the use of the whip, and whether you or M. Hauteville was the first to introduce its pleasures into your married life?"

Again she blushed, and did not immediately speak; and Lady C. repeated her question, when she replied in a low tone, "I was."

"You first taught your husband to find pleasure in whipping?"

"I did."

"And where did you learn it yourself?"

"In the convent where I was brought up."

"Was it practised there as a punishment only, or as a pleasure as well?"

"Both—as a punishment by the sisters and priests, and as a pleasure by the girls of the convent school, who learned the use of the rod from their superiors."

"You have not told your husband of our meeting and your intentions?"

"I have not."

"And you will not?"

There was a difficulty in the answer of this question. Mme. Hauteville would say no more than "Not if I can help it," which caused much laughter and some consternation, though the ladies agreed amongst themselves, that as M. Hauteville practised whipping himself he would not be likely to say anything even if his wife did let the secret out. Whether she did or not, he held his tongue; and I heard my lady remark that he was exceedingly attentive to and careful of her the next day, when she kept her room. The whipping she got was a pretty severe one; the different kinds of instruments used made the punishment harder to bear than the continuous stroke of a single rod, and her poor hips were all weals and bruises. When I took her away to her room Mlle. St. Kitts went with her, and remained in her rooms; she and that lively young lady took a fancy to one another at once, and Mademoiselle sympathised with her in her sufferings. Mlle. St. Kitts was an orphan, or she would never have been admitted. She was staying at the château under the protection of her aunt, Mlle. Loupe, one of the before-mentioned old maids, a cross, strait-laced creature, but quite powerless to control the wayward girl, who was to all intents and purposes her own mistress. She lectured her severely upon her joining "those women," as she called the ladies, and vowed she would make the Count put an end to their secret meetings.

"The Count would be only too glad to join us, auntie," she replied; and indeed, when Mlle. Loupe spoke to him indignantly about the proceedings of the tabagie, he replied that so far from trying to stop the amusements of his guests, he intended to apply for admittance to their meetings himself, for he was sure that what ladies could keep secret with such pertinacity must be intensely interesting and amusing.

Mlle. St. Kitts related all this at the next meeting of the society, to the amusement and indignation of the sisterhood, and added that her aunt was excessively curious about their ceremonies.

"I think the best plan would be to enlighten her," said Mrs. D., with a laugh, and she drew her rod through her fingers as she spoke.

"What, admit her!" said Lady C. "I don't think we should find her an agreeable associate, nor a silent one either."

"I don't think we should; but we might initiate her for all that: let her have a taste of our proceedings, and I don't think she would want any more, or would be likely to go tattling to the Count again. We'll leave Mlle. St. Kitts out of the scheme if she likes."

"Oh no! I owe auntie a grudge for many a bit of spite, and if you don't serve her worse than you served me, I shan't grumble, and she'll be none the worse."

"Half the *whipping* will do, my dear, but I think we can cure her of curiosity, and complaining too," replied Mrs. D.; and then, rising, she begged permission to lay before the meeting a plan of revenge upon Mlle. Loupe for her ill-will towards the society. It was received with much laughter and approbation; and it was resolved that if the lady showed any more animosity it should be immediately carried out. They had not to wait long. The very next day the fair lady again assailed the Count with a request that he would deprive the ladies of the use of the smoking-room, and put down the "disgusting orgies" held there. The Count repeated her words to my lady, and the sisters resolved upon instant revenge. When Mlle.

Loupe retired that night to her room she found a note upon her dressing-table, inviting her to join the rest of the ladies in the tabagie the next evening. It further directed her to knock at the door of the smoking-room at a certain hour *alone*, otherwise she would not be admitted. The note concluded by saying the ladies trusted to be able to convince her of the complete harmlessness of the secret society, about which she had so kindly interested herself. She went to her niece's room in great excitement to know who sent the invitation, but Hilda was mute upon the subject.

"She had heard the ladies express a wish to have her aunt join them," that was all she would say about it; and Mlle. Loupe passed the night and the next day in a state of extreme excitement.

The ladies met that night in their ordinary evening costumes, for reasons which will presently appear, except the two footmen and the page, who were on duty beside Lady C.'s chair. The room was almost in darkness; the only lights were two candles on the stands at the top of the room, and as soon as the knock was heard at the door these were blown out, leaving us in total darkness. This had been arranged beforehand, and the Princess's maid removed from her post of outside doorkeeper. Mrs. D. disguised her voice, which she had a knack of doing, and asked who was there? Mlle. Loupe answered timidly, and was immediately drawn into the room, and the same voice told her she must be blindfolded. In the twinkling of an eye, and before she could resist, her hands were pinioned, and a handkerchief tied over her eyes. While this was being done the candles were lit, and a dozen hands seized upon the unlucky victim. Struggles were vain, screams of no avail; indeed, they were lost in the peals of laughter which resounded on all sides. Mlle. Loupe was prepared, horsed, firmly held on the back of one of the footmen, and soundly whipped. To describe her appearance would be vain. Fancy a scraggy, sallow woman, with skin like parchment, and a coiffure composed mainly of false hair, which loosened itself in her struggles and kept tumbling off; and a shrill voice, which now and then raised itself above the general tumult in a sharp squeal, which was more temper than pain, for the ladies laughed too much to make their blows very hard. A very few minutes sufficed to give each of them an opportunity to use their rods, and then one by one they glided silently from the room. The pins which held up her dress were taken out, and the bandage over her eyes loosened, and she slid to the ground to find herself alone with two men and a page. They stooped over her with well-acted surprise, but she shrieked and hid her face.

"Men, too!" she screamed. "Oh! oh! go away; it only wanted that to complete their wickedness. Go away, I tell you! How dare you come here? Send my maid, you wretches—Mlle. Loupe's maid—oh, oh! they've murdered me."

She was wasting her lamentations on the empty

air, and when she looked up again she was alone.
There was the empty room, not a trace of any occu-
pancy remaining, and she rolled over again on the
couch bewailing her smarts and the way she had
been tricked. She must have lain there some time,
when, getting a little calmer, she sat up upon the
couch and confronted a man gazing at her, no less a
person than the Count's valet, a very fine gentleman
indeed, who had been passing near the tabagie, and
attracted by unusual sounds, had entered, and was
surveying Mlle. Loupe's disarranged dress and disor-
dered coiffure with mingled admiration and astonishment.

"Another man!" she shrieked. "Are you one of
them? Are you leagued with the wretched women
who meet here and indulge in such abominable practices? I have been——" she stopped suddenly, and
said, "insulted, outraged in this room, and I will have
reparation."

"There is no one here but Mademoiselle," the man
replied, puzzled; "the ladies are in the drawing-
room; there has been no meeting in the tabagie tonight."

"No meeting! Do you dare to stand there and tell
me that when I——? Ah! I see you are one of
them; perhaps one of the vile men who was here just
now, hired by those women to insult me."

"I will send Mademoiselle's maid to her," was all
the reply he condescended to make to her, and
walked off to the drawing-room, where, after a little

delay, he was able to speak to his master, and tell him that Mlle. Loupe had gone mad in the smoking-room.

"Is it a secret, Count?" asked the Princess, who had dressed and was moving about the room, delicately lovely in a pale primrose-coloured dress. "Your face looks interesting."

"Does it? It was a serious piece of news André brought me, I can assure you; he says Mlle. Loupe is in the tabagie raving mad. Have you anything to do with this sudden alteration of her intellect?"

"I have done nothing to produce such a catastrophe as that."

"I strongly suspect your sisterhood, who hold the secret conclaves yonder, have been practising upon her amiable nature. Ladies, shall we go and see how far André's dismal tale is true?"

Down in a body went the ladies, with the Count at their head, to gather round Mlle. Loupe, and question and condole with the utmost innocence. She spoke out plainly now, declared she had been shamefully outraged, whipped, and degraded in the presence of his servants, at a secret meeting of the ladies in the château.

"But, my dear madame, there has been no meeting here tonight; the ladies have given us the pleasure of their society in the drawing-room, where we have missed you, I can assure you."

"You have been tricked, and so have I!" she said in a fury. "I tell you I was beaten by two men in livery, and a page stood by and looked on; and I heard the laughter of a room full of people at my sufferings. Count de Floris, if there is law in the land, I will have it!"

"Certainly, my dear madame; if you can point out the offenders, I will aid you to the utmost in bringing them to justice."

"Point them out! They are your guests, these women who think nothing too shameless to indulge in at their vile meetings."

"I think we had better retire, Count," said Mrs. D., with dignity. "Mademoiselle's malady appears to be one for which a night's rest will be the best remedy."

"Dear, dear, how sad!" said the Princess slyly. "I had no idea of anything of that sort; better ring for her maid, poor creature, and have her taken upstairs at once."

The Count was puzzled, and half inclined to think that his guest *had* been indulging too freely in champagne at dinner, but he spoke gently to her. "Indeed, my dear madame, you are under some delusion; if you will allow me to conduct you to your room, the matter will be most carefully investigated."

There was nothing for it but to comply, and the next morning every servant in the house was strictly examined. No one knew anything about it, of course; none of the men had been near the tabagie on the previous night, and the women had only to report that they had dressed their ladies for the evening as usual, with no information regarding any meeting. It's my belief that the Count knew or guessed at the truth, and rather enjoyed the discomfiture of Mlle. Loupe; who, poor soul, remained under the imputation of having taken more wine than was good for her on that particular day, and who never attempted any more to meddle with the other ladies, or to interfere with the doings of Mlle. St. Kitts. It gave her a lesson she did not forget, and she was obliged to take it to heart in secret and without any fuss. She had no witnesses to bring forward, and of course there was only her own word as to the whipping. She could not very well produce ocular proof of the fact, and her assertion did not go for much. She was a much more amiable woman after the little ceremony, which gave her an insight into the doings in the tabagie, than she was before; and it was a long time before she again tried to learn any of the secrets of St. Bridget. When she did—but that is too long a tale to tell now; I'll let you have it in its proper place. My lady is calling, so I must go.—Believe me, as ever,

Your sincere friend,

M. ANSON.

PS—My letter is quite long enough, but I may not be able to write again for some time, and I see I have been scribbling on without ever answering your question about Gustave. My lady only wanted me to give me some orders about her dress for a hunting party

that is to come off next week, where they are all to
be in Moyen Age costumes, and make fools of themselves, by pretending to hunt a poor tame boar that
has been kept in a pen in the woods here ever since
we came. My lady is going in a crimson dress, with
gold trimmings; Mme. Hauteville, in blue and silver;
and the little Princess in green and gold. Old Lady
C. (and what a spectacle that woman will be on
horseback, to be sure!) has composed a costume out
of two old black velvet and satin dresses, and
trimmed them with white and silver like a coffin;
she'll look like an undertaker's advertisement. But all
this has nothing to do with that imp of a page. You
ask whether he took all the punishment he got
quietly, and whether he did not retaliate upon us for
his whippings. Of course he did, and in a way we
little expected, and could not resent. There was a
ball at Tours, a very select and genteel one, and
most of the ladies and gentlemen at the château—
I mean in our circle—were invited. We had some
work to get permission, but as it happened on an
evening when we were not much wanted we did get
it, though I must not tell you how we were haras-
sed till the very last minute, and barely allowed
time to dress and get off. I was fully prepared two or
three days beforehand; as I told you, my foot and
my lady's are the same size, and though she is taller
and stouter than I am, a little alteration makes her
dress fit me. I was resolved not to be outdone in the
matter of dress, and I selected a blue and white shot

137

silk, which had been only twice worn, and Honiton trimmings. There were shoes to match the dress, which my lady did not much like—she always said it did not suit her complexion. It did mine beautifully, and I can tell you that there was quite a buzz of admiration when I walked into the ballroom with M. Pierre, M. Hauteville's valet. For ornaments, I had a garnet and pearl set belonging to my lady, and a perfumed fan, which had just come with a lot of other things from Paris. Fifine had much more trouble with her dress; she was taller and bigger than her little mistress, and she was obliged to content herself with a lace dress as the only one she could alter successfully. *I* helped her with gloves and shoes; and with some Paris diamonds and deep crimson flowers she looked very pretty. Gustave helped with our toilettes, and was very demure and quiet all the evening—so quiet that we could not help fancying he meant mischief.

"I *know* he's up to something," Fifine said, as we drove off. "Oh, Mademoiselle, suppose he was to go to our ladies and tell about these!"

She put her hand up to her neck where her mistress's ornaments glittered, and looked frightened, for the Princess had a temper, and was easily offended.

"Oh, no fear!" I replied. "Gustave is not a bad-hearted boy: he may play us some prank, but he won't do anything deliberately spiteful."

The ball was a most delightful one; we were universally pronounced the belles of the room, and had more attention paid us than any other people of the place. It was late when we got home, and we found that Stephens, good-natured for once, had attended to our duties for us, and we could go to bed at once. Not a sign of Gustave was to be seen; the men said he was in bed long ago, and we went off to our rooms, glad to be rid of him, and tired enough. We undressed and folded up our dresses, which were none the worse, and chatted freely about the ball and what we had seen and done there. All at once I hear a smothered laugh somewhere: I was sure of it, but though we looked well about we could see nothing. Our lights were soon out, and I got into bed. I had left the door open, and could hear Fifine get into hers; a moment more, and she sprang out with a terrified scream.

"What is the matter?" I asked, and then there came a peal of mischievous laughter, and Gustave rushed past me, and in a moment had locked the outer door communicating with the corridor, and taken out the key.

"You little wretch!" I exclaimed. "What do you want? Where were you?"

"In my bed," gasped Fifine. "I—I——"

She could not speak between rage and fright, and the boy, who was half dressed, only laughed the more.

"That's just where I was," he said; "and now, you two girls, look here: I've let you whip me and lead me a precious life, and I'm going to turn the tables. I'm going to whip both of you, and try my hand, or else go straight to the Princess the first thing in the morning and tell her about the fine dresses I helped to put on."

The little brute was quite in earnest. Not only had he been lying in bed in wait for us, but he had two rods there, which I knew at a glance had come from the Princess's store; and do you know, my dear, many things made me fancy afterwards that she knew about it—both the dresses and the whipping too. Well, to make a long story short, and to save myself *I* consented that Gustave should whip me— and the little wretch made me go through all the proper ceremonies, and then gave me as good a flogging as ever my mistress did. Fifine resisted for a long time, but she, like me, knew what he could do to spite us if he chose in other ways besides the ball affair (for we had talked quite unrestrainedly before him), and she submitted at last. How the little wretch chuckled when he got hold of her, and we recovered our breath after the scuffle.

"Now, Mademoiselle," he said, mimicking the Princess's voice to a nicety, "kneel down and kiss the rod!"

Fifine hesitated, but a smart cut across her unprotected legs brought her to reason.

"Let him have his way," I said; "it is no good thwarting him."

So she knelt and did as he bade her, and he lectured her the while with such a serious face that I

140

could not but laugh, though I was smarting I can tell you.

"Mlle. Fifine," he said, "you have been guilty of a grave offence in wearing your mistress's dresses and jewellery; you will now take punishment for the same at my hands. Rise, and lean over the ottoman! Mlle. Anson, hold her hands!"

We both laughed—we could not help it; but Fifine saw it was best to submit, and she took her flogging quietly—the imp of mischief asking her whether it was not much nicer to be whipped by a fine handsome young man (fancy a monkey of fourteen calling himself a man) than by an angry mistress. At length he stopped, and Fifine was as sore as I was; she jumped up and made for the door.

"Oh, I haven't done with either of you!" he said, wickedly; "that was only for the dresses: now about the jewels."

In vain we protested and begged; he declared if we did not do all he required of us he would go to our ladies the first thing in the morning and describe exactly what we had worn. There was nothing for it but to obey, and, standing by the chair where he had whipped us, he ordered us to turn up our nightdresses and fasten them. When we had done this he made us march before him round and round the room, administering alternate cuts to one and the other. I looked at Fifine, and she at me; we had had about enough of it, and when he once more sat down we put our own smarting hips out of the question, and sprang upon him, one on each side. In a twinkling he was down, and his head tied up in towel; then his hands fastened, then his legs, and then he was at our mercy.

"Now it is our turn," Fifine said, while I hastily undid the fastening of his trousers, the only clothing he had on, except his shirt.

"Oh, let me go!" he begged. "I won't tell; indeed, indeed I won't!"

"I don't intend you shall," I replied; "but we shall whip you in case you forget and let a word slip"; and, rolling him over, we administered a full payment for what he had given us. He was not a vindictive fellow, for he never told; and as far as *my* lady was concerned our secret was safe. From a good many little things that slipped out I always fancied that the Princess was not so ignorant either of the dressing or the whipping, but she kept her own council, and we heard no more about it. But I must not write more now, for my lady will be back directly. Let me know when you get this, and believe me,

Your affectionate friend,
M. ANSON.

FANCIFUL FLOGGING

My Dear Marion,

I can quite understand your impatience to hear more from me, but the fact is that after the practical joke the ladies played on Mlle. Loupe they deserted the tabagie for a while. That outraged lady's bewailings, they feared, would draw too much attention to their proceedings. Besides, they felt sure that the Count suspected something, and though they would not restore the room to the gentlemen, they practised in their secret convocations. Poor Mlle. Loupe paid the place many a visit in secret to see if she could discover anything, and so did many of the servants, who enjoyed the story of the whipping immensely (for the victim made no secret of it); but there was nothing to be discovered—the pretty room was just as they left it—dais, crimson chairs, lamps, and all, but no sign of anything to tell of what went on there. As for Gustave, that boy knew pretty well the truth—his own experience had taught him, and the way in which he condoled with Mademoiselle, and offered her his services to help her to discover the culprits, was edifying to see. At first she took it into her head that *he* was the page who had witnessed her humiliation, and meeting him in the corridor one day in the identical ruby velvet suit the Princess had worn, she caught hold of him, and cuffed him, and shook him till his howls brought out his mistress, and one or two more of the ladies, to see what was the matter.

"I assure you, you are mistaken, madame," the Princess said, when the accusation was preferred. "Gustave wears that suit for the first time today! He has never seen it before."

"Oh, haven't I?" the boy said, *sotto voce*, with a comical glance at the petite figure of his lady, who, I fancy, caught the words, though Mlle. Loupe did not.

"But it is the same dress, colour, ornaments, and everything, even to the crest on the buttons."

"There is no crest on the buttons," replied the Princess demurely. "I do not use a crest for Gustave: it is a simple fleur-de-lis which anyone may use if they like."

Mlle. Loupe looked confounded, and the Princess went on in the same grave fashion:

"As to the colour of the dress, it was a fancy of mine, but as it so exactly resembles that of someone else, he shall never wear it again: I like my servants to be unique if possible. For the rest, madame, I shall feel obliged if you will leave Gustave alone for the future; I can correct him myself when there is any occasion for it."

She sailed off in a dignified fashion, so foreign to her general manner that the ladies could scarcely refrain from bursting into peals of laughter; indeed, Mme. Hauteville, who was one of those who were with her, made a most precipitate retreat from the scene, and we could hear her silvery voice in uncontrollable merriment after the door was closed behind her.

As for Gustave, Mlle. Loupe made him a sort of half apology: that is to say, she admitted she had been mistaken, and declared that the page she had seen was not so stout as he was, which was very true. He accepted her apology, and vowed he would help her to find out the truth, which coming to the ears of the ladies through Mlle. St. Kitts, they had him up to my lady's dressing-room, and whipped him in full conclave, every lady using a different instrument, as had been done in Mme. Hauteville's case. He was sore enough afterwards, and made no more proffers of assistance to Mlle. Loupe. My lady did not relish the cessation of the whipping festivities; it was a pastime she delighted in, and I can assure you, my dear, that I suffered from her enforced abstinence from her favourite recreation. She used to practise upon me to keep her hand in, and she was no mean performer with her pet instrument, I can tell you.

She had a dozen ways of indulging her fancy, always at my expense, and one of them was peculiarly aggravating.

She got hold of a great book out of the library,

which had a history of feminine manners and customs in ancient Rome (and nice manners they must have been), and she resolved to make me attend upon her toilet as the slaves of the Roman ladies did. So she looked up a short tunic which was among the fancy dresses, and the next morning she made me go and strip, and come back to her with nothing on but this garment, which was just like a sack, with short sleeves only, of soft white merino, trimmed with red satin. It did not come to my knees, and my legs and feet were bare, except for a pair of sandals of red leather.

"Now take care what you are about, Anson," she said. "I am going to deal with you exactly as the ladies in Rome dealt with their slaves."

"But I am not a slave, my lady," I said, impertinently enough, I dare say, for I felt angry. "There are no slaves here."

"You are mine as long as you are in my room," she replied. "When my toilet is sufficiently completed, I shall punish you for that speech." She made me bathe her, and perfume her, and dress her hair, and then before she put on her stays she said quite calmly, "Bring the rod." I brought it, and she made me kneel and kiss it, and beg her pardon for what I had said; and then I knelt over the couch, and she whipped me till she was tired, and I, well, I did not get over it for a long time. For a good while after that she made me attend her in that detestable tunic; and how the boy Gustave used to jeer and laugh

about it to be sure! But I had some fun out of it too,
for Lady C. heard of it, and took a fancy to have
Stephens do the same; but the sight of her skinny
yellow legs was too much for her mistress and such of
the ladies as saw her, and after one sound whipping
she was let off. The way that she lamented and
anointed herself after she was whipped was very
funny. The ladies teased her unmercifully, and took a
delight in getting her punished; they knew her legs
were a sore point with her, poor soul. But though my
lady languished for the use of the rod, she was not
alone in her longing, and on the second day after the
meetings ceased there was quite a gathering of ladies
in her rooms. I knew quite well what they were come
for, and was not at all surprised when my lady told
me to lock the door. They were all *en peignoir*, and
were certain of an hour or two to themselves, the
gentlemen being engaged with their own pursuits,
and most of them out of doors. Mlle. St. Kitts was
among them; they had all taken a fancy to her, and
indeed, she was first and foremost in all their frolics;
she was dressed in a white muslin robe, trimmed with
fine lace and amber satin ribbon; my lady was in
pink, and Mrs. D. in blue; the little Princess was all
in white, and Lady C. in a hideous old flannel dressing-gown that looked as though it had been fifty
times washed. They were all anxious for a little practice with the rod, and despatched me to the chamber
of the Princess for the necessary weapons. She kept
them in a long box, lined with velvet; and splendid

rods they were, lithe and well tied, regular stingers, not like the clumsy things we used to make up when you and I were girls together. When I returned with them, I found the ladies in full gossip; they were questioning Mlle. St. Kitts as to where she learnt anything of the use of the rod, and that lively young lady did not scruple to relate her experiences for their benefit.

"I've been used to it all my life," she said, in answer to a question from my lady; "ever since I can remember I have been accustomed to see whipping. My father had a whipping house on the estate, and we used regularly to go and see the slaves whipped, especially the girls; they were stripped and tied up, not horsed like——"

"Like you were," said my lady with a laugh. "Confess, my dear Miss St. Kitts, were you not frightened out of your wits?"

"I was; I thought for a moment that you really had introduced the male element, but auntie's fright has atoned to me for mine."

"Does Mlle. Loupe still think it was the servants?" asked Lady C.

"That she does, and wants the Count to have a police inquiry."

"Which he knows better than to do. I dare say she was not *always* so frightened of a man."

"No, that she wasn't. I've heard mamma tell stories of her younger days; and when she was at St. Kitts no one took more interest in the whippings. I've

148

seen her take a rod myself in the slaves' dining-room,
and she has whipped me often; she was considered
an elegant hand."

"Ah," said Lady C., "there is a great difference in
the style of whipping. There is no enjoyment either
in the use or endurance of the rod when it is vulgarly
used, like a woman would strike in a passion; but
when an elegant, high-bred woman wields it with
dignity of mien and grace of attitude, then both the
practice and suffering becomes a real pleasure."

"That is just what our governess and the nuns at
the convent school used to say," said Miss St. Kitts,
her eyes flashing and her cheeks glowing at the
recollection; "and they let us feel it, too.

"Ah, I've had some convent experiences, too,"
laughed the lovely little Princess. "Lay that box
down, Anson; though Mademoiselle here is impatient
to feel one of those dainty weapons, she will have to
wait—we are going to have our gossip out first."

"Am I to be the victim?" asked Mlle. St. Kitts; "I
had no notice."

"Yet you came prepared, I know," said Mrs. D.,
merrily lifting the girl's skirts as she spoke, and dis-
playing the shapely brown legs and slim ankles of the
West Indian heiress. She had nothing on under her
peignoir but an embroidered petticoat and a fine chemise, and her feet were thrust into quilted satin slippers.

"Convicted," she said. "What say you, ladies; shall
not she be whipped, being ready?"

"Agreed, agreed!" responded the ladies, laying hands on the plump West Indian, with looks of delight.

"Oh, a truce, a truce!" exclaimed Mademoiselle. "Fair play, ladies! I plead guilty to having come ready, but have you not all done the same? I propose that the one to be whipped should be the one who has *not* thought of preparation, not those who have."

The ladies laughed and agreed, and a general examination ensued, when, lo! it turned out that the Princess Z. was the only one who had come unprepared for the ceremony. In vain she pleaded that she had come in a hurry, that there had been no notice given her, etc.; she was ordered into my lady's bedroom to prepare, while the ladies gossiped and chattered among themselves.

"Your whippings are child's play compared to our school punishment," Miss St. Kitts remarked. "The sisters used to pick the bits of birch out of our skins for us after a severe flogging, and the priests used to scold them for it, and tell us that those prickles were part of our penance."

"Ah!" said Mrs. D., twitching uneasily on her chair; "that's carrying matters too far. Did those worthy gentlemen help at the punishment, my dear?"

"As far as looking on was an assistance, they did. The sisters professed to do it in private, but there was a sliding panel between the refectory and the room of penance, and they could apply their eyes to it if they chose."

"And you may be sure they did choose."

"Oh, we know they did, but we got used to it; besides, we had to walk through the refectory prepared for punishment, where the whole school was assembled—Lady Superior, nuns, confessors, and all—and they made us walk very slowly, too."

"Prepared?" said Lady C.

"Yes; this sort of thing," said the lively girl, giving her drapery a dexterous twitch up over her shoulders, and assuming a most comical expression of face, as, with her arms crossed, she walked slowly through the room. The sight of her plump, round hips and smooth, firm flesh which the action disclosed was too much for my lady, and, slyly seizing a rod which lay beside her, she gave the young lady a smart cut with it, which made her jump and sit flat down on the floor, amid the laughter of them all.

"That's not the way to receive punishment," said Lady C., when their mirth had subsided. "This meeting do agree that Mlle. Hilda St. Kitts shall stand up and submit to such chastisement as the sisters shall think proper for such an undignified proceeding."

Which Miss St. Kitts did, and folding her hands, humbly begged that the punishment might not be too severe, so that she should not be able to partake of any fun which might come after, and she was condemned to walk up and down the room twice, prepared for punishment, and to receive or elude as she could the blows from the ladies' rods. This proceeding ended in a romp, and I don't think Miss St. Kitts got much hurt, for she looked so funny with her pretty morning robe pinned up round her neck, and her brown legs contrasting so oddly with her snowy chemise, that the ladies laughed too much to be very mischievous. Just as their fun was at its height the Princess entered, having removed all her under-clothing. When the turmoil had a little subsided, and the heiress lay breathless and rolling on the floor, she presented the rod, and kneeling to Lady C. begged for punishment. The Countess, my mistress, and Mrs. D. voted for a few minutes' pause; they were out of breath, as, indeed, were all the ladies.

"Then let someone tell a story," said Lady C. "Princess, you are the only one of us with breath enough; entertain us while we rest."

"As a ransom? Will you take a story and let me go free?" asked the little lady, who, truth to tell, did not much care for the whipping, having, as she confided to my mistress, been taken to task by her husband on one occasion as to the meaning of sundry marks on her white skin. He had been at the château during a visit he paid to Paris, and was expected again for a day before returning to St. Petersburg, and his appearance was curiously ill-timed, having taken place on the day following a grand meeting of the ladies, at which the Princess had come in for a full share of the rites of St. Bridget.

"What say you, ladies? Shall the Princess ransom

herself?" Lady C. asked. "Far be it from us to make His Highness uncomfortable when he comes to visit his lovely wife, or to make conjugal differences through our secrets."

"Oh, we never differ," the Princess said, laughing. "Michael is afflicted with curiosity, that is all, and he knows I never do penance, so it was awkward to answer him. What must the story be about?"

"Something bearing on the rod, its use, etc.—some of your own experiences."

"I haven't any," she said, ruefully; "I told you so when I first joined you."

"I have it," said Mrs. D. "Let us consider the Princess absolved if she can tell us quite a new story about whipping—something we have not heard before."

"Perhaps Mrs. D. will take my burden off my shoulders," she said, comically; "she looks full of stories."

"No, Princess! no shifting," said my lady; a story from *you*, or the rod."

"I *do* know something!" she replied, her face brightening; "but it is not my own experience, it is my grandmother's."

"No matter, so it is new to us; can we take a hint, any of us?"

"You might give your husbands one," she said laughing. "A lady could not undertake such a matter very well."

"Is Anson to hear it?" asked my lady.

"Oh, anyone may hear it who is bound to keep our secrets. Anson, fetch me a shawl: this costume is slightly cold."

I fetched a soft wrap, and she curled herself up in a corner of the soft couch like a dormouse, with nothing out but her head and the point of her tiny slippers. She was a luxurious little creature, and loved warmth, and soft cushions, and perfumes, and lace, and all the graceful appliances of her rank, very dearly. I think to strip her of them would have been to kill her.

"My story is about my grandmother when she was a schoolgirl," she said. "She was an Englishwoman, and educated at a school of the first fashion, near Bristol. She married afterwards the Marquis de Bearne, but that has nothing to do with my story."

"I'm afraid it won't be very original, Princess," Lady C. said. "School punishments are all alike— kissing the rod, asking pardon, and the rest of it."

"There was something unique about this one, any-way," she replied; "and I think you'll all acknow-ledge it when you have heard it."

But the Princess's tale was too long for this letter, Marion. My mistress is to be out tomorrow the whole day, and I will try and take up the story of the flogg-ing ladies then, and let you hear what amused them all immensely.—Meantime, believe me, as ever,

Your sincere friend,

M. ANSON.

THE PRINCESS'S STORY

My Dear Marion,

I will try to take up my story where I left off, and tell you the tale the Princess related to the ladies to save herself from a whipping. Everyone is out—gone to a Watteau picnic in the grounds—so I have a little time to myself. It was an odd story she told, and sounded very like a page out of a romance, but she vouched for its truth; and Mrs. D., when she had done, corroborated it, having heard something of the sort from her own mother.

"I have the whole story in grandmamma's own hand somewhere," the Princess said, "but it is in Paris, so you must be content with it as I can tell it. She was a very dashing girl, of about nineteen, when it occurred, so you may well imagine it made an impression on her. There were no private governesses in those days, and families of the first fashion and highest station sent their daughters to school. That of Miss K., at Clifton, was one of the most celebrated and select; she received no ladies but those of the highest birth : not even clergymen of any grade under a bishop could get their daughters admitted. The number was limited to twenty, and the rate of payment was very high. My grandmother had a list of what the young ladies were required to take with them in the way of toilet, and it was most expensive and *recherché*. Carriages were kept for the use of the scholars; and they appeared every evening in full dress. It was essentially a finishing school, fourteen being the very earliest age at which a young lady could be admitted, and many remaining there until they left to be married. To fall in love was not permitted to an English demoiselle in those days: all was arranged by her parents. Clifton was a secluded place then, and select—not a vulgar showy watering-place as it is now—and the school stood alone. Miss K. was a rigid disciplinarian, and the punishment of the rod was enforced for every offence; the pupils submitted to it as a matter of course, and getting many a lesson in the manner of wielding it from their elegant preceptress, who had quite a reputation for the grace with which she inflicted punishment on the young ladies under her care.

"One morning, while they were at their studies, a carriage and four dashed up to the gate; this was no unusual apparition, as there were no railways in those days, and the parents of many of the pupils travelled in that manner, and the young ladies usually arrived at Cliff House and departed therefrom in great style. Miss K. was in the schoolroom, but she made no movement to go to see who the new arrival might be; she stood on her dignity, and waited for his card to be brought to her. The scholars nearest the window saw a tall, elegant man step out of the carriage, which was most handsomely appointed, and enter the house. In a few minutes the footman brought in a card on a salver and presented it to his mistress; it bore a crest and the name of Sir Arthur Kempe, and, in the corner, in very small letters, 'Inspector of Schools under His Majesty's Commission,' surmounted by the Royal Arms.

"Miss K. looked at it a moment in a little perplexity, and then at her scholars.

" 'Young ladies,' she said, 'this is a gentleman to inspect the school; go to your dressing-rooms all of you and take off your morning dresses. A quarter of an hour is allowed for the change.'

"She rang the bell, and ordered the maids who attended to the toilettes of the pupils to be at their posts, and the girls filed off to their respective chambers to change their dresses. The morning dress at Cliff House was a sort of uniform of white muslin and lace, trimmed with pink or blue ribbon, according to the complexion of the wearer, and this was worn till the hour of the midday lunch, when they were changed for walking costumes, and these again for dinner dresses later in the day. But little time was lost over dressing; the young ladies were taught promptitude and neatness, and a very few minutes sufficed for the change of attire. While the girls went to their rooms, full of curiosity as to the new arrival, and wondering whether they were to be subjected to any examination, Miss K. was closeted with the stranger in her private apartment. He greeted her with a bow of the latest fashion, full of grace and dignity, and took care to display his fine figure to the best advantage. He wore a dark plum-coloured coat and breeches, and an embroidered vest of canary colour; his ruffles were of the finest lace, and his stockings of the most delicate shade of pink silk; he wore his own hair, tied at the back in a queue. His appearance was slightly effeminate and dandyish, but his manner that of a complete gentleman.

" 'I have not the honour,' " Miss K. began.

" '——Of knowing me? No, madame,' he replied; 'but I rejoice thus to commence an acquaintance with a lady so widely known and respected as Miss K. I bear his Majesty's commission, madame, to make a somewhat delicate investigation into the state of ladies' schools in this realm. I trust you will give me all the assistance in your power.'

" 'Certainly,' Miss K. replied; 'I court inspection in my establishment, and have ever done so.'

" 'My mission, madame, is to inquire into the punishments in use in the various schools. There has been a great deal of discussion in London lately as to the use of the rod in ladies' schools; and my commission empowers me to inquire how far it is used, the effect of it, and, if I deem it necessary, to see impending punishment inflicted.'

"Miss K. looked somewhat aghast at the announcement; she had never heard of such an official proceeding as this, and she hardly knew what to say.

" 'Allow me to show you my credentials,' he said, taking a flat leather case from his pocket, and producing a parchment deed. It was regularly endorsed, and bore the King's sign and seal, and empowered Sir Arthur Kempe to enquire into the discipline of the ladies' schools all over the kingdom, and declared that any lady who refused information would be liable to condign punishment on being reported by 'His Majesty's Commissioner.'

" 'I am perplexed,' the governess remarked, when she had read the parchment. 'I use the rod, of course, and my pupils submit to it when necessary; but I do not know whether they would yield to any examination or punishment from another.'

" 'If they do not, madame, your school will be ruined. I have found most of the ladies whom I have visited amenable to reason. In the last house I called at, Mrs. J., of Mark Villa, Gloucester, I found the discipline too slight, and was present at the punishment of no less than six young ladies. The *verbal* orders I received, in addition to yonder document, were very stringent, I assure you."

" 'How do you wish to proceed?'

" 'Assemble your school, madame. Let me see your black book : I shall examine into the condition of pupils after punishment, and superintend the next whipping. If discipline is properly exercised (and I am sure it is),' he added, with a bow, 'you will hear nothing more of me or my commission; if not, why, I

shall have to put a black mark against you, as you
do against your pupils.'

"There was nothing for it but to lead the way to
the schoolroom, where, by this time, the pupils were
all assembled, and introduce her guest. They rose and
curtseyed at his entrance, and he saluted them with
easy grace, and took his stand by the governess's
desk, who explained to her pupils, not without some
trepidation, the object of his visit. One of the younger girls was ordered to fetch the black book and the
rod, which she presented kneeling, and the gentleman
turned over its pages.

" 'Angeline Summers,' he read, 'corrected yesterday for inattention and untidiness. In the usual way,
madame?'

" 'In the usual way, Sir Arthur.'

" 'Prepare the young lady, and allow me to see the
effect of the punishment.'

"Now Angeline Summers was a fat roly-poly girl
of fifteen, or thereabouts, who was always getting
whipped. She did not care about the rod, not she,
but she did about the presence of this stranger, and
she flatly refused to let her weals and stripes be exhi-
bited to him. But he was firm, as became a man in
authority; and Miss Summers was securely held by
two of the maids, and her silk dress turned up over
her head. She bore the marks of plenty of whipping,
and Sir Arthur Kempe declared himself satisfied, and
the young lady was released and sent off to arrange

her dishevelled hair, with another whipping in prospect for having been so restive.

"Another girl's name was then read out, a tall, slight, plain girl this time, who had been whipped but slightly that morning for some trifling offence. She resisted very little when ordered to prepare, for she had sense enough to see that Miss Summers only made matters worse by kicking and struggling; and, though she put up her hands to hide her burning face, she said nothing, but allowed her clothes to be turned up in silence.

" 'The punishment in this case has been very slight,' the commissioner remarked. What was the offence?'

" 'Insubordination and neglect of duty,' was the answer : 'two black marks.'

" 'It should have been at least double, Miss K. Allow me.'

"And, taking the rod from her with a bow and a smile, which half the girls present would have thought cheaply bought by a whipping, he administered some half dozen cuts to the shrinking figure before him, which made the culprit shrink and writhe more than Miss K. had ever done. When she had been released he turned to the book again.

" 'There is one name down for punishment I see,' he said; 'Emily Saltère, for neglect of duty. Which of these ladies is Emily Saltère, madame?'

"All eyes were turned to my grandmother, whose handsome face turned scarlet, and there was no need to answer his question. He started as he saw a tall, handsome young woman curtsey, with the grace of a Parisienne, as he mentioned her name, and, stepping forward, he bowed to her with much respect.

" 'I regret, mademoiselle,' he said, gracefully, 'that my duties should take a form disagreeable to you, but I am bound to attend to them. Madame, I desire to see the punishment carried out exactly as it is always performed in your establishment—omit nothing, and add nothing, if you please.'

"Miss K., with a trembling voice, gave the order—

" 'Arrange yourself for punishment, young ladies. Prepare Miss Saltère.'

"Miss K. signalled to the attendant, but before she could turn up the handsome dress my grandmother wore, Sir Arthur Kempe interfered.

" 'I think, madame, with your permission, that I will break through the rule of public punishment in this instance, and have the punishment inflicted in another room; I have no wish to hurt the young lady's feelings *more* than is necessary. My duty compels me to be an unwilling witness of the chastisement, but I do not desire to make it harsher than is needful.'

" 'Remove Miss Saltère to the drawing-room,' Miss K. said, much relieved; and my grandmother was led away to her bedroom, where she was stripped, and taken back to the drawing-room in her chemise and a delicately frilled dressing-gown, trimmed with costly lace. Sir Arthur Kempe bowed to her as she entered,

and himself handed her the rod, which she delivered
to Miss K. kneeling, and was bidden to kiss. Then
her dress was carefully pinned up, leaving her completely bare, and she was made to lean over a large
ottoman while the governess whipped her. Miss K.
was generally severe, but her agitation on this occasion made her strokes fall lightly, and punishment,
though somewhat tedious, was not severe. The gentleman watched the performance with critical eyes, for
my grandmother was a well-formed, plump girl, with
a fine clear complexion and healthy skin. He compli-
mented both mistress and pupil on the manner in
which the whole thing had been gone through, and
himself handed Miss Saltère to the door, kissing her
hand as she left the room. He made an entry of a
report in his book, which already held many such,
and assured Miss K. that he should speak in the very
highest terms at headquarters respecting her select
establishment. He stayed to dinner, insisted on the
rest of the day being given to the pupils for recreation, and departed for the next school on his route,
having won golden opinions from all in the house, in
spite of his unpleasant errand. The following morning Miss K. received two or three letters from ladies
who kept schools asking if she too had been visited,
and describing the beauty of the novel commission.
Some time after my grandmother received a visit
from her aunt, the wife of a dignitary in the Church,
to whom she told what had happened; and inquiries
were made which led to the discovery that the

elegant gentleman who had visited the schools and had the young ladies whipped for his delectation was not Sir Arthur Kempe at all, but an Earl's brother who had taken this extraordinary method of gratifying his passion for the rod. It was all hushed up for the sake of the many young ladies concerned; but the story got wind, and many schools fell into disrepute through it.

"And that's my story, ladies," said the lively little Princess; "and I think it is something new in the history of the rod."

But I must break off here, Marion, and leave what followed for my next.

Your sincere friend,

M. ANSON.

A PROFITABLE PUPIL

My Dear Marion,

I left off the other day at the conclusion of the story the Princess Z. told, which the ladies received with much laughter and applause. She made it so piquant by her charming manner and pretty imitation of the different people she talked about that they were all delighted, and unanimous in declaring she should be considered to have ransomed herself from her whipping.

"I think that *is* something *new*," Lady C. said; "I don't fancy any of us can equal that in our experiences."

"And it is *true*," Mrs. D. added; "my mother's school received a similar visitation. I have heard her speak of it, though I had forgotten it until now. But, ladies, time flies; who is the next——"

"Victim, eh?" said Miss St. Kitts, gaily. "Why, you, dear Mrs. D., of course. How say you, sisters, shall Mrs. D. be now whipped?"

"Oh, yes, yes," they cried, seizing upon the plump lady, who was fat, fair, and nearer forty than thirty, and preparing to turn up her richly trimmed peignoir

165

over her head. "Yes, Mrs. D. by all means; she does not get her fair share of the rites!"

I saw my lady draw her rod through her fingers, as if she relished the idea of letting it fall smartly on the plump white flesh of the buxom Mrs D., who was as comely and wholesome-looking a lady as I ever saw. Her limbs were as firm and round as those of the youngest of the whipping sisterhood, and a rich healthy tinge showed under her clear skin, the result of a sound constitution and regular habits. Mrs. D. never left her bed in the morning without plunging into a cold bath, and braced her system with regular exercise, which she never omitted, whatever the weather might be. She was a large woman, tall and inclined to be stout—had she been indolent she would have become corpulent; as it was she was just fleshy enough to be handsome, and to give the idea of perfect health, which, indeed, she enjoyed. She had regular features, blue eyes, and white teeth, which ill-natured people declared were not her own, so perfect were they in preservation. She had an abundance of silky hair of a very pale shade of brown, not light enough for flaxen, nor brilliant enough to be called golden; its slight tinge of red preserved it from insipidity, and, wound round her handsome head in a style peculiar to herself, it was at once striking and beautiful. Mrs. D.'s passion for the rod was intense; she never missed an opportunity of witnessing or practising the use of it. To do her justice, she never shirked it from the hands of the other ladies, and more than once I have led her away from the tabagie and assisted her to bed after a severe whipping, for her maid was not in the secrets of the meetings. She was always ready for her share of the fun, but on this occasion, to the surprise of the ladies, she demurred.

"Not this morning," she said, laughing, twisting herself free of their detaining hands, and shaking down her peignoir over her plump legs. "Like the Princess I call a truce; I will take my punishment at our meeting tomorrow night, but not now."

"Why not?" demanded Lady C. "A good reason, mind, or the punishment will be doubled."

"Well, then," said the lively lady, "time flies; our lords and masters will soon be in, and we must present ourselves in the drawing-room in trim array. Dinner time is drawing on, and I, for one, should not like to go down smarting and twisting from the effects of the rod; what say you, ladies? Is not my reason sufficient?"

They all agreed that it was, and that it would be better to defer any further practice of the rod till the next night, when they were again going to meet in the tabagie; but Mrs. D. was informed that she must follow the example of the Princess, and tell a story relating in some way to the practice of whipping.

"I have none of my own experience," she said. "Whipping is all the same wherever practised, but I could tell something about a lady I once knew, once upon a time."

"Oh, don't go back into remote ages!" said the little Princess; "let us have a story of our own days."

"It is not so very long ago; did I not say I knew the lady? It all happened when I was a girl. I was living, with my parents at E——, when there suddenly appeared in society there a rich, or apparently rich, widow, Mrs. A. She lived in good style, kept her carriage, and had a handsomely appointed house and plenty of well-trained servants. No one knew the source of her wealth or where she came from, but she rapidly became popular in the best society, and by her dashing manner and splendid appearance won for herself an eminent position in the fashionable world. Like many fine ladies, she cherished a secret passion for the rod, and odd stories began to circulate, through the medium of her maids, of the way she used it on herself and them. But flogging her maids was poor pastime for Mrs. A., who, report said, had been accustomed to use the rod upon her husband very freely, and she cast about in her own mind for a victim fresh at once to the practice and to her. Fortune came to her, and in rather a strange way. The back windows of her handsome house looked across the corner of the square towards the rear of a row of houses somewhat less pretentious, some of which were let out in aristocratic apartments. In one of these lodged a Mr. B., a young gentleman of immense fortune, and some two or three and twenty years of age. At twenty-five he was to come into absolute possession of his estates and property, and in the meantime he was studying, under the care of a guardian, at the university at E——. That someone should overlook his studies and pursuits was necessary from the fact that he was slightly weak in his intellect—not enough to make him unable to study, or sufficient to render him an object of remark, but so much so as to make it necessary that his inclinations to extravagance and propensity for childish display should be controlled. One night, when Mrs. A. was retiring to rest, she accidently cast her eyes towards a window on the ground floor of a house opposite, where Mr. B., thinking himself unseen, was preparing for bed. She watched him for a long time, for the young gentleman, fancying himself unseen, indulged in a variety of pranks, by no means disagreeable to the eyes of a sensual woman, like the lady who sat at her darkened window looking on. In the morning Mrs. A. took up her post of observation again, and found that the light streamed full into the room the young man occupied, and discovered him lying undressed upon the sofa with a book. A powerful opera glass disclosed every object in the room with the utmost distinctness, and showed her the tastes and habits of its owner. She could discern two or three German books on the table, the very simplest of grammars, such as a child might use, and one or two rough exercises evidently written by a beginner. Now Mrs. A. was an accomplished linguist, and she saw in this circumstance a way to make the young man's acquaintance, for his handsome face and fine

169

form had inflamed her with a strange desire to know
him. Again the next night she watched, and had
ample opportunity of studying the stranger's perfection of form and limb, and she resolved to set about
making his acquaintance the very next day. He was a
singularly handsome young fellow, blue-eyed and
fair-haired, and a very Apollo in form. The lady was
fertile in expedients, and the next morning despatched her maid to inquire if there were apartments to
let in the house where he lived. She was informed
there were, and Mrs. A. immediately proceeded to
inspect them "on behalf of a friend." Of course she
wanted no rooms, but the landlady, garrulous after
the fashion of her class, gave her unasked all that she
did want—viz., information respecting her lodger.
She could speak of his wealth and his prospects, and
tell who he associated with, and where he visited, etc.
Mrs. A. learned that he had but few friends, and no
young men companions of his own age, which was
rather pleasant for her to hear. One of the houses he
frequented was one of which she herself had the
entrée, and she resolved that she would meet him
there. A little dexterous questioning, not unaided by
the universal talisman of money, made her as *au fait*
to the young man's habits as the landlady's tongue
could make her, and she returned home to wait once
more for the evening, when she might again watch
him alone in his luxurious room. He was evidently
possessed of taste as well as wealth, and his apartments were furnished with everything that could con-

duce to his comfort or appeal to the sensual tastes she
had already discovered he possessed. Again she was
able to remark him unseen, and feast her eyes upon
the form and proportions which had so taken her
fancy, and she retired to rest more than ever determined to lose no time in obtaining an interview with
him. Chance favoured her project, cards of invitation
arrived for a select party at the house of the mutual
acquaintance, and she found to her delight that Mr.
B. was invited too. She dressed herself to the best
advantage (she was, as I have said, a splendid
woman), donned her handsomest jewellery, and set
out, bent on conquest. The introduction was soon
made, and she knew at once what course to pursue.
If Mr. B. was free and easy in his conduct in the
privacy of his own apartments, he was shy to a fault
in company. Almost painfully awkward, he shrank
from conversation, and seemed fully conscious of the
slight defect which existed in his mental organization.
Mrs. A. saw this, and set herself to draw him out as
only an accomplished and self-possessed woman can.
In an hour he had forgotten his shyness, and was
sitting by her side chatting with perfect freedom of
himself and his pursuits. He talked to her with the
utmost confidence, told her of his studies and how
trying he found them, and she listened and sympathised till he grew quite bewildered with her kindness
and intoxicated with her beauty and fascination. It
was so rarely that ladies cared to talk to him
much—he lacked the graces which make a young

man's society agreeable to the fair sex, but Mrs. A.
resolved that he should not lack them long. She
pondered over some way to find an excuse for inviting
him to her house, and he supplied it himself, by
confiding to her that, of all his studies, the German
language puzzled and tormented him most. Now, she
was an excellent linguist; she had a natural gift in
acquiring languages, and, having spent years abroad,
spoke French and German like a native. Here was an
opening. She at once proffered her services, declared
so much more could be done by conversation than by
poring over books, and invited the delighted youth to
come and take lessons of her. Before the evening was
over he was completely captive to her charms, and,
when her carriage came round, and he was permitted to wrap her costly shawl round her handsome
shoulders, and to draw the overshoes on her shapely
feet, his hands trembled so he could hardly perform
the pleasant little duties gentlemen delight to take
upon themselves for pretty women. He hardly waited
till noon next day had passed before he presented
himself at her house, where he was most cordially
received. From that hour his subjugation was complete: Mrs. A. might have done anything with him,
and she made full use of the advantage she had
gained. He became a constant visitor at her house,
her follower wherever she went, while she, on her part,
was rather proud of exhibiting the faithful attach-
ment of her handsome Adonis. Unlike the beautiful
youth of Venus's adoration, he was nothing loath to

pay back, in her own coin, the attentions she lavished on him. For a long time it came to nothing more than untiring attention on his part, and flattering condescension and fascinating smiles and witcheries on hers. But servants will be servants, and ere long a whispered rumour got afloat that there was more in their acquaintance than mere politeness. Mrs. A. began to wear handsomer jewellery than ever, and more fine dresses and silk stockings found their way into the possession of her maid than formerly. The daily visits went on, and Mr. B.'s infatuation grew greater than ever for the well-developed charms of his idol. He was happy in obeying her slightest whim, delighted to be allowed to fetch her shawl, or her dainty slippers, when she chose to sit with him for a cosy chat. The excuse for all this was *German lessons*, Mrs. A.'s services as teacher being well appreciated by her well-grown pupil. But somehow it soon began to be whispered that other matters besides German teaching were attended to in these frequent *tête-à-têtes* which took place in the lady's boudoir. The room was fitted up in the most voluptuous style, with amber satin hangings to suit the dark style of her beauty, and white lace to interpose between them and the too fair complexions of some of her visitors. Pictures of the most suggestive kind covered the walls, and helped to increase the infatuation of the youth, who, from the moment that he entered the house, seemed completely carried away by the sensuous splendour around him. The boudoir had an unused door, opening into a spare room, behind which Mrs. A.'s maid used to ensconce herself, and, without the knowledge of her mistress, became a silent witness of the sort of teaching that went on. Before her acquaintance with Mr. B., her lady was a splendid dresser, but now she became more luxurious than ever. One time she would appear before the enamoured youth in a *négligé* costume trimmed with the most costly lace, made so that every movement displayed her handsome bust or rounded arms; at another she would dress herself in full evening costume, and meet him under the soft light of the lamps, with every surrounding that could appeal to the senses or excite the imagination. One toilet, which caused no small sensation at more than one party that winter, figured afterwards in the bills sent in to Mr. B.'s guardian. It was composed of green velvet of a tint peculiarly becoming to the brunette complexion of Mrs. A., and was trimmed with the rarest lace to be procured in E——, which was set down, by the draper who supplied it, as "fifty yards, at two guineas per yard." From dressing to receive her pupil, the lady soon got to threatening him with punishment if he failed in his lessons. At first it was all a joke.

" 'You deserve to be whipped,' she would say; and down he would go on his knees, and kiss her white hands, and clasp his arms around her to caress away her anger, while she submitted to his endearments, nothing loath. After a few encounters of this sort affairs grew more serious, and her fancy for whipping her interesting pupil could be restrained no longer.

" 'I shall whip you this time,' she said at last, after a more than usually blundering performance of her scholar.

" 'Not this time,' pleaded he, casting himself at her feet, and clasping her plump, white hands, which he covered with kisses.

" 'Yes, now! Stand up, and take down your trousers.'

" 'No, no! I will try and do better; I will indeed.'

" 'No excuses, sir,' she said, with feigned severity, while the maid listened intently, and marked how her eyes flashed with excitement. 'At *once*, sir,' and she took off her dainty slipper, affording more than a glimpse of her handsome leg as she did so. The young man fell at her feet, and embraced them, and kissed them; but it was all to no purpose—she was inexorable : she made him undress, and bestowed upon him a smart slapping with the slipper she held. But this only gave her a more decided zest for the rod; and when she informed her scholar that the *next* time he transgressed he should be whipped with a *rod*, and severely, too, he kissed her hands and her rosy mouth, and intimated that he was ready to submit to anything she chose to do with him. The maid held her tongue about this, but not about the more ceremonious whipping which took place shortly after, and of which she was also a witness. Before Mr. B. arrived, she was ordered to fetch a box out of her

mistress's dressing-room, the contents of which she
was very well acquainted with, and place it in the
boudoir. This she did, and then took up her post of
observation. The young gentleman came as usual,
and began his studies, blundering egregiously in a
very short time. She made him stand before her like a
little boy, lectured him severely on his carelessness,
and ordered him to bring the rod. In vain he begged
and prayed, kneeling before her, and kissing her feet,
covered only by a thin silk stocking. She commanded
him to stand up and prepare, which he did, still
begging and praying to be released. Mrs. A. would
have no mercy, and his trousers were quickly taken
off. Then he was bidden to bring the rod, then to kiss
it, and finally, the lady laying him across her knee,
administered a thorough whipping, till he fell on the
floor, smarting and exhausted. All this the maid saw,
not once, but many times, and, after the fashion of
her class, did *not* hold her tongue about it. The result
of all this was that Mr. B. grew so wildly in love with
his fair instructress, that he became in danger of
ruining himself for her. There was no limit to his
extravagance, and Mrs. A. was a lady of expensive
tastes. Gifts of all sorts began to find their way to her
house. Gems which he would swear could not rival
the lustre of her eyes; dainty slippers which he would
fit on, and kiss the exquisitely shaped foot they were
made to adorn; articles of vertu, and sumptuous
feminine adornments of all sorts, were almost daily
delivered at her door, and the affair became a matter

of public scandal. The guardian of the infatuated young man remonstrated with him on his extravagance without effect, until a bill for £2000, for a parure of emeralds, opened their eyes to the true state of the case, and they refused to pay for the jewels. Mrs. A. as stoutly refused to give them up, and the result was an exposure of the circumstance, which resulted in Mr. B. being at once despatched to his estates in Ireland, and the lady having to make a hasty retreat to 'fresh fields and pastures new,' where she might perchance pick up another wealthy innocent to minister to her whims and passions."

"And is that all true?" Miss St. Kitts asked, when Mrs. D. had stopped.

"Quite, my dear; I remember the lady perfectly, and a handsome creature she was, just the style that boys fall in love with. But come, ladies, we have not much time before dinner; I vote an adjournment till tomorrow night."

They all agreed and dispersed. I'll write again and tell you about that other meeting in the tabagie, which, as it happened, was the last.—Meantime,

I am,

Your sincere friend,
M. ANSON.

"WHICH ENDS THIS STRANGE EVENTFUL HISTORY"

MY DEAR MARION,

I have only one more meeting in the tabagie to tell you about, for, as it befell, the ladies were discovered, and my lord was so indignant that he insisted on my lady leaving the château at once. The day after they met in my mistress's dressing-room for the private practice I told you about, there was to be a grand meeting at which they intended to hold a perfect festival of flogging. Everyone was to flog and be flogged in turn, and the dresses they were to wear were to be of the most piquant and expensive description. Every lady was to go prepared to submit to a whipping; and those who wore male attire were enjoined to put on nothing underneath but a fine chemise. Two ladies dressed as footmen, and one as a page; Mlle. St. Kitts as a savage, and very handsome she looked. She had a white chemise hanging very loosely over the bosom, with pendant gold coins along the edge of it; a cashmere shawl of brilliant orange colour curiously disposed about her by way of drapery, and a tiger skin thrown over her shoulders.

179

The shawl, which had a beautifully embroidered border of all the colours of the rainbow, served her at once for skirt and scarf, and was draped in a very picturesque manner. Nearly the whole of one leg was bare, and the other was seen up to the knee; her feet were thrust into sandals made out of the skin of a panther, or some skin dyed to represent it; and her hair was suffered to flow as loosely as such a curly crop could be made to do, and was adorned with a fillet of pendant gold coins the same as those on her bodice. She made a charming picture as she walked up the room with the free undulating grace so remarkable in her movements, and the ladies all murmured their admiration. The little Princess elected to represent Ariel for this night only and looked a study for a painter with her round bare limbs and soft white drapery. The dress was very low and short, hardly reaching to her knee, and was confined round the waist and across the shoulders with bands of gold. A diamond star formed the buckle of her belt, and another glittered on her forehead, held there by a secret fastening, which made it quiver and shake like a living thing over her glossy hair, which fell in rippling masses to her waist. *My* lady chose to go in the Pompadour costume, which suited her style well; and Lady C., like a stingy old thing, as she always was, went as a Lady Superior of some convent or other, in a costume of grey stuff and white flannel, with a string of wooden beads, and a crucifix which never cost above half-a-crown, I am sure. Mrs. D. at first

thought of being a gentleman, but, as she said afterwards, it was next to impossible to cram her fat
proportions into any sort of men's clothes, so she gave
up the idea, and appeared in a sort of Dame Durden
costume, with a steeple-crowned hat, high-heeled
shoes, scarlet petticoat, black bodice, and point lace.
She looked very funny with her fine hair all stuffed
away under a mob-cap, and spectacles on her good-
humoured-looking face, and the ladies laughed
immensely at her and her costume. As for Stephens
and myself, we were ordered to dress like two charity
girls, with caps, mittens, and aprons all complete, and
nice figures we looked, I can tell you—one in red,
and one in blue. I was almost forgetting Mme.
Hauteville's toilet for this grand night; she went as a
Vivandière, and bewitching she looked. Her skirt was
of bright scarlet silk, soft and noiseless, with bands of
velvet, and buttons down one side exactly as you see
it in the opera, only that every button was a cluster
of diamonds worth a little fortune; her jacket was of
blue velvet, with scarlet facings, buttoned with diamonds; a tiny white linen collar stood up round her
full throat, and dainty white gauntlets covered her
little hands. She had rolled up her splendid hair into
somewhat masculine-looking curls, and wore a grey
felt hat with a splendid ostrich feather, fastened by a
diamond aigrette in front. Her boots were of soft
black kid, and her legs were bare—the dress being
short enough to show about half of the calf of her
leg. She made a lovely addition to the varied picture

the bright dresses presented as she walked up the room and a hearty burst of applause greeted her appearance.

The room was decorated with the prettiest flowers, and I had a day's work helping my lady and the Princess to tie the rods afresh with different coloured ribbons. The weather was intensely warm, and the skylight of the tabagie was left open till the very last moment, for the sake of the air. It fastened on the inside, and could be opened and shut at will by anyone in the room; it was of opaque glass, and effectually kept out prying eyes even if anyone could have got up there to look. When the ladies were all assembled, each with her rod, and Lady C. in her place on the dais, as president, she bade me shut the window.

"Ah, is it necessary?" Mrs. D. asked with a shrug. "We shall melt, as well as smart, before the evening is over."

"Consider, madame," Lady C. replied, "if we leave the window open, we are at anyone's or everyone's mercy. Even in such an apparently inaccessible place it would be dangerous to leave a loophole."

"I fancy the only spies would be cats and sparrows," the Princess said, with a laugh; "but Madame la Présidente is right. We had better be sure; so shut the window, Anson, and fasten it so that no inquisitive folk may lift it up."

I loosened the cord, and the heavy skylight came down with a bang, shutting out the glimpse of the

starlit sky we had before seen, and I stood upon a
chair to make it fast. I felt sure, as I did so, that the
rope did not come to its usual place upon the hooks;
that the window, in short, was not quite shut. I
looked up, but it appeared closed; and as no pulling
of mine could make any difference, I just held my
tongue, and fastened it. It was no business of mine,
and no one could get up there to peep, so it did not
signify much. The proceedings of that meeting were
somewhat different from those which had gone
before; the ladies wanted a fresh sensation, and they
resolved to have it. Instead of one of the sisterhood
being horsed and whipped, or running the gauntlet of
all the ladies' rods, each one was to whip her next
neighbour; in fact, a round robin of flogging, with
neither beginning nor end. Previous to this, Mrs D.
was to take the punishment she had promised not to
shirk, and then, after a short interval for her reco-
very, she was to be the centre figure of the next
performance, and give the signal for the blows to be
struck, which were to be given with the precision of
clockwork. The lady being duly prepared, she was
found too big to be horsed, and, amid the laughter of
the ladies, she was escorted by the two footmen to the
square ottoman in the middle of the room, over
which she was made to kneel, held by the supposed
livery men, while the page handed the rod. There
was a great deal of tittering over the performance,
for she looked very funny in her mob-cap, with her
old woman's dress turned up, and her tall hat on the

floor in front of the ottoman. Lady C., too, looked extremely grotesque in her nun's costume, whipping away with all her might, with the perspiration washing the rouge down her face in red lines. While all this was going on, I fancied—nay, I was sure—that I heard a curious noise something like a groan, though where it came from I could not tell. Looking round I saw, from the startled face of some of the ladies, that they had heard it too.

"What is that?" said the Princess. "Where did that noise come from?"

No one could tell, and though every nook and corner of the room was searched, and the two outer rooms explored, no way of accounting for the noise could be found. The skylight was fast, and, after a moment or two of confusion, the alarm subsided, and the ladies prepared for the universal whipping they had planned. They arranged themselves all round the room after a short interval, during which they partook of champagne and biscuits, and cooled themselves a little with perfume from a pretty fountain, which was one of the latest additions to the luxury of the smoking-room. I was placed in front of Lady C., and I shivered as I thought of how she could hit, and Stephens before the little Princess, who did not much like her, and whose tiny hands could deal a stinging blow. Mrs. D. was seated in the middle on the ottoman over which she had been whipped, and when they were all ready she gave the word "Prepare!"

Up went the dresses simultaneously, but the "gentlemen" found more difficulty with their costumes, and there was not a little laughing, which caused peals of merriment. At length, however, the buttons were mastered, and the nether garments turned down; the gentlemen were in place and position, and Mrs. D. gave the word, "Strike!"

Every rod was uplifted, but ere they could fall there came a slight shriek, and an unmistakably feminine voice exclaimed, in cracked tones—

"Oh, the disgusting monsters! Oh, the abandoned wretches!"

A peal of irrepressible laughter from another voice followed and accompanied the words, and the ladies gazed at one another in amazement and consternation. Ere they could recover their scattered wits, another catastrophe occurred; a sudden crash, as of some heavy body falling on the flat roof, was heard, and a hand dashed through the skylight, scattering the glass in all directions, and admitting a rush of cold air. Screams and howls succeeded to this catastrophe, through which we could still catch the sound of laughing, smothered this time, as though stifled with a handkerchief, and then a pair of lightly shod feet pattered lightly away over the roof.

"Out with the lights," said Lady C., "and then to your rooms, ladies; we have had spies upon us. Let everyone dress as quickly as possible, and appear in the drawing-room."

Out went the lights in a moment, and not an

instant too soon, for the screams and cries of the person on the roof brought plenty to her aid. Feet sounded over our heads, and sympathising voices mingled with exclamations of amazement and alarm.

"Not a word," whispered Lady C., "and remember, dress as you were dressed before; we must be presentable before many minutes are past. Away at once, and silently."

You may be sure we lost no time in obeying her orders, and, seizing our cloaks from the anterooms, we rushed off. We met several of the guests and servants, who asked what was the matter, which no one seemed to know; and the Count and several of the gentlemen were nowhere to be found. Mlle. St. Kitts came to my mistress's room to dress, and very quick she was about it, for not many minutes elapsed before she was ready for any emergency. It was fortunate for her, for there came a knock at the door, and the Count's voice was heard enquiring for her. Something seemed to have affected him powerfully for he was shaking with suppressed laughter, and could hardly speak. Mademoiselle went out to him, and left the door open, so that we heard the conversation. The Count looked surprised to see her dressed, and made her a low bow.

"Will you come to your aunt, mademoiselle?" he said. "She has met with a slight accident."

The young girl looked him in the face without blenching, though her eyes twinkled.

"Poor auntie!" she said. "She seems unfortunate. What has happened to her?"

"She has cut her hand rather badly with some broken glass; any other information she will give you herself."

He spoke gravely enough; but their eyes met, and the girl's uncontrollable spirit of fun burst out in a hearty peal of laughter, in which he joined. She saw that he knew it all, and she put a bold face on the matter.

"What extraordinary gymnastics my aunt must have practised tonight," she said demurely, after their laughter had somewhat subsided. "Did you assist her, Count?"

"No, on my honour," he replied, as they walked away.

My lady was too frightened to laugh at what had happened.

"That old cat," she said, when she had heard all; "she must have had some crack to peep through. Anson, we are undone; she is quite capable of holding a levée of gentlemen, and telling them everything."

Which I have no doubt, from the sequel, she did. I was dreadfully frightened and angry too, and I took an opportunity of getting away to seek Gustave, who, I felt sure, had been the mover and helper of Mlle. Loupe's scheme. If my vengeance was swift, someone else's was swifter, for I came upon M. Hauteville in the corridor dragging him by his collar, and in a very few minutes indescribable yells issued from his apartments. I saw no more of Gustave, for I had enough on my hands before long, but I heard all about it afterwards. He and Mlle. Loupe between them had concocted a plan by which to get on the roof of the smoking-room, which they carried out by means of a ladder purloined from the garden. How she must have bribed him, to be sure, before he joined her in her freak. He had better have peeped by himself, for the discovery led to his instant dismissal by his mistress. However, he didn't lose much by that, for my lady heard afterwards of his being seen in Paris in the train of the little golden-haired Mme. Hauteville.

Within an hour from Mlle. Loupe's summons to her niece, my lord came to my lady's dressing-room, and had a long talk with her. He never got into a passion, but he was very decided. All I heard was, "Julia, you will be ready to leave this place at six o'clock to tomorrow morning," and then he came to me in the bedroom.

"Anson," he said, "you will pack up all your mistress's and your own things, and be ready to leave here the first thing in the morning. I shall take the early train to Paris."

I curtseyed, of course, and he went on—

"I don't know how far to blame you for the disgusting business which was accidentally discovered tonight, so I will take the most charitable view of the case, and suppose you to be a mere tool in the hands of others. For your lady's sake, I will not dismiss you now, but warn you to be careful of your conduct for the future."

And that was all, my dear. We were hustled off in the morning without being allowed to see any of the other guests. The Count accepted the plea of sudden and particular business, and gave me a billet de banque for a hundred francs, when he bade me good-bye. I heard afterwards that Mlle. Loupe had a bad hand for a long time (and serve her right, the nasty prying thing!), and that Mlle. St. Kitts got so tired of her tyranny that she ran away from her to her guardian in Paris. But there were no more meetings in the tabagie, and the Order of St. Bridget was broken up. And that's how we come to be vegetating here in England, with my lord as cross and stiff as you can imagine, and my lady low-spirited and dull. Write again, and believe me as ever,

Your sincere friend,

M. ANSON.